LOST IN THE CITY

The Texas Pan American Series

LOST in the CITY

Tree of Desire and *Serafín*

Two novels by Ignacio Solares

• • • • • • • • • • • • • • • •

Translated by Carolyn & John Brushwood

 University of Texas Press • Austin

Library of Congress Cataloging-in-Publication Data

Solares, Ignacio, 1945–
    [Arbol del deseo. English]
    Lost in the city : two novels / by Ignacio Solares ;
translated by Carolyn and John Brushwood.
        p.   cm. — (The Texas Pan American series)
    Contents: Tree of desire — Serafín.
    ISBN 0-292-77731-0 (cloth : alk. paper). —
ISBN 0-292-77732-9 (paper : alk. paper)
    1. Solares, Ignacio, 1945–   —Translations into
English.   I. Brushwood, Carolyn.   II. Brushwood,
John Stubbs, 1920– .   III. Solares, Ignacio, 1945–
Serafín. English.   IV. Title.   V. Series.
PQ7298.29.044A8613   1998
863—dc21   97-35001

CONTENTS

PREFACE

Ignacio Solares is a major figure in contemporary Mexican literature: the author of a dozen novels and several plays (some based on his novels), editor of the cultural supplement to the weekly magazine *Siempre,* and director of the Department of Literature at the National University of Mexico (UNAM). His awards and honors include two fellowships at the Centro Mexicano de Escritores (1975, 1977), the Magda Donato Prize (1988), the Diana/Novedades International Prize (1991), the National Prize for Cultural Journalism (1993), membership on the National Council for Culture and the Arts (CNCA, since 1994), and a Guggenheim fellowship (1996).

Life in Mexico City—you might even say the life *of* Mexico City—is basic material in Solares' novels. They are stories of personal relationships sensitively detailed, with natural dialogue and the use of special effects that may be called "supernatural" (not the "magical realism" so often noted in Latin American fiction). In more recent novels, Solares adds a historical dimension by focusing on the experiences of some of Mexico's revolutionary leaders, the great figures that defined the political beginnings of modern Mexico. Intensely human, credible characters inhabit all of these narratives.

Solares was born in Ciudad Juárez in 1945, but he has never been a regional novelist. Rather, both his life and his interpretation of Mexico seem to extend outward from the capital city, always recognizing the centrality of that sprawling mass of humanity. His first novel, *Puerta del cielo* (1976), focuses on a young man of modest background who works as a bellboy in a Mexico City hotel. Outward relationships are interwoven with the protagonist's inward realities and, surprisingly, with visits from the Holy Virgin. This kind of supernatural effect became a hallmark of Solares' novels. He followed the first novel with a documentary narrative about alcohol-induced visions (*Delirium tremens*, 1979). His next novel, *Anónimo* (1980), opens with the startling statement "It seems laughable, but that night I woke up being somebody else." This novel proceeds to test the limits of reality in ways that may remind readers of the play and film *Heaven Can Wait.*

During the 1980s, Solares produced three notable novellas: *El árbol del deseo* (*Tree of Desire*), *Serafín,* and *La fórmula de la inmortalidad.* Each of the three stories features a juvenile protagonist who is quite real, and some kind of supernatural effect (such as telepathy). Late in the decade, Solares published a major novel about twentieth-century Mexico City, *Casas de encantamiento* (1987), that folds three time periods into each other, thereby projecting certain essential qualities of the place.

Near the end of the decade, Solares published his first historical/ political novel, *Madero, el otro* (1989). This story deals with the conflict between idealism and political expediency in the leadership of President Madero. (Solares discovered that Madero communicated supernaturally with a deceased younger brother.) The success of this novel led to others featuring historical figures: one about Felipe Angeles (1991), another about an archetypal post-revolution president (*El gran elector,* 1993; presented on stage in 1991), and a third about the invasion of the United States by the forces of Pancho Villa (*Columbus,* 1996). Another well-known figure, Plutarco Elías Calles, is the protagonist of one of Solares' plays (*El jefe máximo,* 1991).

Published in 1994, Solares' *Nen, la inútil* returns to the time of the Spanish conquest of Mexico. Nen, an Aztec girl, is raped by a young *conquistador* who could have had her as a willing lover. This incident is a metaphor for the convergence of the two cultures as perceived by Solares. Here, as in all his work, he seeks an understanding of the society in which he is an important actor.

◆ ◆ ◆ ◆

In the two novellas translated here, *Tree of Desire* and *Serafín,* Solares demonstrates his particular adeptness at portraying the complex lives of young people—an unusual subject in contemporary Latin American fiction. Cristina, the ten-year-old protagonist of *Tree of Desire,* runs away from a home that is outwardly normal but inwardly dysfunctional. She takes her four-year-old brother with her, and confronts some of the humbler and more troubling aspects of life in Mexico City. Or is it all a dream? If it is a dream, Cristina also dreams within that dream. Solares' narrative, deceptively simple on its surface, suggests that the terrifying city may be a metaphor of Cristina's life within the family, a nightmare that may not come to an end with the end of the story.

Serafín, in the novel that bears his name, is a boy (eleven or twelve years old) who lives in rural Mexico. His father has left the family for Mexico City, taking the village beauty with him. Serafín's mother sends the boy, by himself, to look for his father. Woven into this story of cruelty and compassion, of connections maintained and broken, is an account of a failed protest march against the injustices suffered by rural Mexicans. In portraying the homespun intellectual leader of this movement, Solares explores the social and economic background that has led to Serafín's plight.

Serafín's world intersects Cristina's, but does not parallel it. Her story moves from middle-class to lower-class within Mexico City; Serafín's story instead moves from a rural to an urban environment. The two novels, read together, offer a multidimensional view of contemporary life in Mexico.

TREE OF DESIRE

For Myrna

1 **"Papá?"**

She woke up frightened, the way she used to when Papá and Mamá had to take her to sleep with them because as soon as they put out the light, she saw faces in the window, heard the door to the street open, and death came to sit at the foot of the bed.

Only now it was Papá's shouting that awakened her.

"Papá?"

Maybe they didn't hear her. It seemed to her the shouts and the dry thud of steps came out of the depths of the dream, and again the nightmare's cobweb extended one of its threads into the reality and dimness of the room.

She rubbed her eyelids.

Sometimes rubbing her eyelids and letting her eyes get used to the faint light from the street filtering through the mesh curtains was enough for her to discover the world was calm, and turn quietly to sleep again, burying herself in the pillow's foam.

But not that night. On the contrary, it seemed every shout—really just one, that echoed into many—suddenly brought back images supposedly forgotten: a shout with the feverish face of a man climbing the stairs holding a bloody knife in his hand; a shout with the livid face of a condemned man looking at her through the window as if begging her to pray for him; a shout with the face of death now sitting in the chair next to her bed, smiling.

"Hi, Cristy, been a long time since we've seen each other."

And Cristina screamed:

"Papá!"

The silence that followed her scream made her think, yes, it was a nightmare that had lasted beyond her sleep. But a moment later Mamá entered, stepping as quietly as a cat, and came over to the bed—her eyes swollen, damp. She told her, please go back to sleep, nothing was happening, she and Papá were talking but now they were going to bed. Cristina didn't answer, but after looking at her carefully, pulled the covers over her head, and hardly heard her mother's last words, my precious little girl, sleep well; tomorrow you have to get up early to go to school, my darling. She heard her leave the bedroom, dragging her feet. Cristina lowered the covers. Mamá had left behind a large shadow, leaning over, her hands lifted up like wings. It did not go away, as though separated from her, the real image of Mamá.

She got up fearfully, as if breaking a serious rule, and went to open the door. Turning the handle slowly so they wouldn't hear it, she opened the door slightly and looked through the crack into the dining room at the scene she already knew well, that she had dreamed and imagined and now became real—Papá walking around and around the table, waving his hands. And Mamá seated with her elbows on the table, covering her eyes, sobbing. Papá was gradually raising the tone of his voice, his words bouncing all over the room, his yelling as much a part of her as her first memories, her first images of the world. And Mamá, daring to answer from time to time with a brief sentence, burning and sharp, like an arrow seeking his heart, which inflamed him even more.

It seemed to Cristina her parents were awakening a volcano that would end up destroying them. She put her hands over her ears and squeezed her eyelids shut. Closing the door with a hard push, she ran back to bed, holding back a sob. She covered her head with the pillow, and the sob turned into convulsive, uncontrolled weeping that choked her and made the pillow stick to her face. Maybe Mamá had come back to ask her to calm down and maybe Papá, too, but Cristina heard only herself; her crying filled the world. She kept the pillow on her face as she was slowly falling asleep, and her weeping died down, becoming sighs that sounded as if she were breathless, imprisoned by her own dreams.

2 **The next morning** she awoke with the feeling of having slept only an instant. The light of day seemed even sadder to her than the darkness. She got up, flannel gown down to her ankles, and looked fearfully for a moment over her shoulder at herself in the mirror on the closet door, as if she were an apparition, a small ghost. She opened the door slightly and looked through the crack, like the night before, but the dining room was empty. The chair where Mamá had sat was a little apart from the table, and the ashtray was full of cigarette butts. The windows to the street were open, and yet, although they weren't there, she had the feeling something was still going on, like the sound of her father's shouting or her mother's sobbing, the atmosphere of conflict, something indestructible. She went through the hall to her parents' bedroom, her bare feet stepping softly on the parquet floor. Any noise might reawaken the volcano. But their door was open, and their beds made up. Hadn't they slept here? Their absence startled her more than if she had found them still fighting. "Papá!" she cried, looking all around as if he might appear suddenly, from where she least expected, perhaps filtering through the wall. She went into the hall and again cried, "Papá!" Her little brother's bedroom was on her right. She opened the door carefully and looked in. The boy was sleeping peacefully in his crib, a corner of the blanket clutched in his hand near his mouth. Feeling more at ease, she went back to the dining room and looked for a note on the table, anything. But there was nothing. Only an empty cigarette pack, an ashtray, and a damp, crumpled Kleenex. She went to the kitchen, the roof garden, the bathroom. Exactly the same. She looked at the clock in the dining room. Seven-thirty. The time when Mamá started getting her ready for school. What had happened? What was she going to do? Stopping for a moment in front of the window in the dining room, she looked at a pale blue, peaceful sky and thought, there's no other way. But she was afraid. Or no, not afraid. A strange sensation, a mixture of fear and pleasure.

She went to her bedroom and, taking off her nightgown, looked in the closet for a dress and some shoes. In the bathroom she splashed some warm water on her face. She went back to brush her hair in front of the light walnut vanity. (Her grandmother had left the bedroom furniture to her, and the moment she saw herself in the vanity mirror, knowing it belonged to her, she felt she was no longer the same, that time was doing a somersault and putting her somewhere else, ahead of or behind the place she had always been.) With a plastic clip in the shape of a tiny flower, she caught up the lock of hair that fell across her forehead and looked at herself sideways, smiling, as always, when she finished dressing. She made her bed and put a rag doll with long hair on the pillows.

"I'm going away, Virginia, take care of yourself."

She went into Joaquín's room and felt the most afraid while watching him sleep. Strength seemed to be leaving her body. Maybe it would be better to wait . . . sleep a while longer, to see what was happening when she woke up . . . But no. It was settled. Period. She touched the child's shoulder gently.

The boy moved around in his bed, squirming and pushing the covers with his feet. Cristina patted his shoulder.

"Come on, honey, we have to go."

He sat up in bed, rubbing his eyelids, not understanding, as if opening his eyes for the very first time. His sister picked him up, put him on a chair, and started unbuttoning his pajamas.

"Where's my mamá?"

"She went away," Cristina answered, taking off his shirt.

"Where did she go?"

"I don't know. You and I are going away, too."

"And my papá?"

"He's gone away, too."

The child said "Oh," and let her take him to the bathroom, where his sister washed his face, put some pants and a clean shirt on him, and combed his hair, making a perfect part on one side. Then they went to the kitchen, and Cristina put a pan with two eggs on the stove to boil and poured two glasses of milk. The child looked at her surprised.

"Are we going to school?"

"No."

"Where are we going, Sissy?"

"You'll see," Cristina replied, breaking the shell of an egg with the edge of a spoon.

"I want to go to school."

"Here, drink this."

He obeyed. Cristina wiped off his mouth, and then put the cups and glasses in the sink and the bottle of milk in the refrigerator.

"Let's go."

"I'm going to get Lucas."

"You're not going to take Lucas."

"Yes!"

"No!"

The child let out such a shrill scream Cristina had to close her eyes sadly and ask herself if it wouldn't be better to give up, to play with Lucas, too, to open the new jar of preserves. They had just given her a very beautiful game of Chinese checkers. Mamá and Papá would come back, they were so good . . . but no (and no), she raised her hand to quiet her brother and, above all, to stop the temptations that doubt was awakening in her.

"O.K., take him. But we have to go now."

The cry—that betrayed a real tragedy—dissolved in a moment and left eyes full of sparks, as if a thick cloud had swiftly crossed the sun. Joaquín came back from the roof garden with a broad smile, carrying the cat by its back with his hand like a set of small tongs.

"I've already told you not to carry him that way. You're going to kill him."

"He likes it."

"What a boy!"

She went to her bedroom for coats and sweaters and—she had almost forgotten it—took a ten-peso bill from the back of a drawer beneath her underwear. She put it carefully in her small red purse, which she wore across her chest like a cartridge belt.

Opening the door to the street, she knew she would never come back there. "Some day one has to leave," she told herself.

3 **They went out** into a sunny morning. Cristina was seeing things as if for the first time, with the sense of creating the world. Before crossing each street, she waited until no car was coming, looking nervously one way and then the other. Then she ran, holding the child by the arm and stopping when they reached the sidewalk, as if it were a recently won beachhead.

"Are we going to school?"

"I've already told you we're not going to school"—the tone of her voice rising—"and carry that cat carefully."

They got to Insurgentes Avenue and stopped at the corner. Cristina was looking at the buses streaming by in front of her, wondering which one she should take. She had gone to Alicia's house with Mamá so many times. Why hadn't she paid attention to the names of things then? Why hadn't she thought she would need to go there someday alone? Now it seemed so hard to remember . . . She took a chance with a very serious-looking lady who was protecting herself from the sun with a brilliantly colored parasol. She looked at them surprised from her square of shade, as if from far away, and asked about their mother. Cristina replied that they were just going to meet her, and chose to walk to the next block to get away from the woman (she had such eyes . . .).

When the bus stopped, she ran to get on it. First she pushed the child on by his waist, and then she got on herself. But she faced a finger moving from side to side like a windshield wiper.

"That cat can't get on," the driver said firmly.

"It's Lucas," Joaquín explained.

A very tall, smiling man took his hand off the chrome bar, stroked the child's head, and then looked at Cristina.

"Please, Mister," Cristina begged the driver.

"Animals can't get on. Come on, get down," and he started to move the gear shift.

Cristina got off first, thinking it would be easier to lift Joaquín down afterward. But he was afraid to jump down from the platform—before the anguished cry of his sister—and the cat must have caught his fright because it slipped out of his arms and ran down the aisle of the bus with Joaquín behind it. Cristina was in the street, with her hand out, pleading, and the last things she could hear were her brother's cries, mixed with the even sharper shrieks of a woman probably terrified by the presence of the animal. An instant later, she saw the red stripe pass in front of her like the flash from a gun, and the roar of the motor was again deafening.

"Joaquín!"

The world spun around dizzily, and everything seemed senseless. She ran with the conviction that if she lost her brother, she would throw herself under the wheels of the next passing car. A cry within drowned her voice:

"Joaquín!"

But the bus stopped in the middle of the block. The air could be breathed again. Cristina saw the tall man who had stroked his hair descend and receive Joaquín and the cat in his arms. He settled them carefully on the sidewalk, smiled and waved good-bye to Cristina, and got back on.

Their coats had fallen, and she had to go back to get them. Then, although still panting and crying, she hugged her brother.

"He scratched a lady," Joaquín informed her, stroking Lucas' head gently.

"Well, I'm sick and tired of your blasted cat. Didn't you see how I ran behind the bus? I almost died . . . What if I'd never seen you again?"

"Oh."

"Besides, they're not going to let us get on with him. Understand?"

The child raised his free hand to his eyes, and his lips became round, but he stopped when he heard his sister's threat:

"Look, if you cry, I'm going to hit you . . . hard, Joaquín."

 They found a solution: put the cat in a plastic bag Cristina got out of a trash can. She would carry it herself, hidden under the coats.

She waited for a bus that was not too full and put Joaquín on first; he never took his eyes off the swinging bag his sister was carrying.

"Hang on really tight to this bar. Here, keep still," she ordered as she gave the ten-peso bill to the driver. She put away the tickets and the change, six silver coins jingling together making quite a noise, with so many. Lucas moved around in the bag, and Joaquín looked at it caressingly. He stayed firmly attached to the bar with both hands, as if clinging to a topmast in a heavy storm.

"Get on, get on!" the driver shouted. "There's room in the rear!"

Then Lucas escaped from the bag with a leap and a meow, as if they had kept him under water for a long time. He ran down the aisle again between cries of fright and laughter.

"He's our cat," Cristina told the driver.

"Go get him." Without looking at her, he began to speed up.

"Can we stay?"

He didn't answer and, preferring not to insist, she went with Joaquín to find Lucas.

They ran the gauntlet of piercing looks and found the cat crouched with flaming eyes underneath the last seat.

"Get that thing out of here!" ordered the woman who, until the moment before his arrival, had been seated where Lucas was, and who was now swaying dangerously with a basket on her arm, grasping for the bar and catching only air.

"He's going to scratch you! He's frantic!" a shrill voice cried from a nearby seat.

However, Joaquín disappeared under the seat, as if diving into a swimming pool, and came up all smiles, holding Lucas up high.

"I told you not to pick him up that way!" Cristina protested and took advantage of the incident to occupy the two seats, in the face of the murderous looks of the woman with the basket.

Joaquín insisted on occupying the window seat, but his sister explained she had to watch the streets to avoid going too far. So he climbed on top of her, because he wanted to look out and show things to Lucas—whom he was carrying with both hands, as if he were a baby—"Look, a bicycle, a dog, a popsicle cart," with a peal of laughter for each discovery. Cristina told herself, Patience, Cristina, and decided to put him on her lap and continue the game, showing amusement at his discoveries.

For a while nobody occupied the next seat (the woman with the

12

basket had found one farther up), so she put the coats there. She had to move them when a very fair, blonde woman, wearing a black suit and smelling of perfume, asked:

"May I sit here, little girl?"

So Cristina put everything on her knees. The woman gave her a friendly smile that the girl ignored.

"Do you know where to get off?" Cristina nodded her head without taking her eyes off the window. The boy, on the other hand, exchanged smiles with the woman, who ended up patting his cheek with the tips of her fingers.

"What a handsome boy. And what a pretty cat," although she did not dare pat it.

"He's Lucas," Joaquín told her.

"Lucas? Like the one in the comics?"

"No. Another Lucas."

"Where are you going, child?"

The boy looked at his sister.

"Keetee knows."

"How old are you?"

With difficulty, the boy managed to separate four fingers and hold them up.

"This much."

"And your sister?"

The child looked at his hands, helpless. Cristina pointed out a motorcycle to distract him. The woman's interest bothered her. What business was it of hers? The boy let himself be intrigued by the attractions outside and forgot their neighbor, who became silent and looked straight ahead. When she got off, Cristina sighed with relief. The seat was occupied by a large man, who began reading his paper.

As they went farther along, Cristina's anxiety increased. How far should they go? And had they passed Sanborn's, the only reference point she remembered? Why did everything—every wall, every house, every store—look strange to her?

When she saw Sanborn's, she jumped and cried, "There it is," pointing her finger at it. The boy was startled and didn't know where to look. Stumbling, Cristina got up, dragging Joaquín along.

13

The man reading the paper grunted as he watched them climb over him. The bus was full, and it was hard to move forward. Fortunately, there was still a block to go. Cristina asked a young man to pull the stop cord and, in a commanding tone, told Joaquín not to let go of her. Joaquín answered yes to everything, staggering, his eyes frightened. With one hand he held Lucas tightly, and with the other he clutched his sister's dress as she pulled him along or pushed him back brusquely. At a sudden jolt they almost fell, and Lucas meowed because Joaquín was smothering him. The door produced a blast of air as it opened. A huge, protecting hand reached over to support them and then help them get off, holding the child (and the cat) while Cristina jumped to the sidewalk. Cristina called out "Thanks," but couldn't see the face.

5 **It was very early;** Alicia would be in school until one o'clock, and they had to pass some time. There was a park on the other side of the street, and Cristina waited for the red light before crossing. She sat on a bench while the boy played with Lucas on the grass, rolling over, laughing, and meowing together as if they were two boys or two cats. Christina told him, Don't do that, be careful not to get dirty, but it was useless, and she didn't insist. She sat with her hands in her lap, looking up and thinking. If she could get some money, they would go far away, as far away as possible. She had to see how much Alicia had. She had offered it to her: when you need it, I've kept my allowance for a year. Alicia was her best friend. Once they had sworn friendship until death. Or beyond death. They had written their pact on a piece of paper and signed it with a mixture of their blood, the way they had seen it done in a film they'd watched together.

Joaquín's cry roused her. Cristina ran to him and took Lucas down from the tree an instant before he would have been dead.

"Joaquín!"

"I couldn't get him down." He wept and covered the cat with kisses and saliva.

"Where did you get this cord!"

"It was here."

"But why did you hang him?"

"He wanted me to."

"What a child, I'm fed up with you." And she pulled him over to a bench. A little later Joaquín was asleep on her lap, hugging Lucas. Cristina shielded his eyes from the sun and looked at him for a long time, her eyes smiling.

She was there for more than an hour, almost motionless, stroking the child's back, watching the people go by, thinking over what to do. She asked what time it was and awakened Joaquín. They crossed Insurgentes again, carefully but running, her heart leaping up in her throat. He wanted some water, and they stopped at a stand to get some pop.

"I want some candy, too," he said.

Cristina asked for a few pieces of gum and took the money out of her purse. They went up a narrow, endless street. The child got tired every few moments, and Cristina tried to carry him, but he was too heavy, so she decided to stop and sit briefly on the sidewalk. Joaquín took advantage of the time to open another piece of gum and share it with Lucas. Finally, after walking for more than half an hour, they saw the two-story house with a huge door, a bronze knocker, and a number at the side. With the tip of her fingers, Cristina reached the knocker and let it fall. A girl with a white apron opened the door.

"Please tell Alicia I'm here. She knows why."

The girl lifted a permanently crimped lock of hair and looked at her with expressionless eyes.

"And your Mamá?"

"We came alone. But . . . we're going soon."

Still without expression, the girl disappeared down the hall and a moment later Alicia came running, still wearing her blue school uniform.

"We left home. I need you to lend me that money from your allowance."

Alicia opened her eyes so wide they filled her face.

"You told me whenever I might want it . . . Remember . . ."

At a distance a demanding voice sounded: Aliciaaa.

"I'll go get it."

Cristina looked into the house curiously, trying to hear. But nothing could be heard, and she only managed to see the two chairs covered in a floral pattern, the sofa, the small table in the center of the entryway, and the hall with columns and paintings of pastoral scenes. Alicia returned panting.

"Here it is," and she gave her three hundred-peso bills. "Mamá changed it for me."

"Did you tell her?"

Cristina saw the tall shadow behind her, like a big black bird with open wings.

"She asked me, and I had to tell her. But she says she understands. And she promised me she won't tell your parents."

Cristina was afraid, and scenes crisscrossed inside her. If she tried to run, the woman would come from behind the door to grab them with hands like claws.

"Come on, let's go," she said, taking Joaquín's hand.

"Really, she promised me."

Then the woman came out from behind the door and Cristina let out a cry that startled Joaquín.

"Cristy."

The woman smiled with very white, sparkling teeth. She wore her hair piled on top of her head and had fat hands with long, red nails.

"Come in, Cristy. I promised Alicia we wouldn't tell your parents."

"That's why I told her," Alicia added as they went down the hall.

They passed by a long dining room with mahogany furniture. There were blue plates on the walls. Alicia's father was seated at the head of the table, his expression solemn, unchanging. When the children entered, he stopped eating, holding his spoon in front of his plate. In the center of the table was a bowl with bananas, apples, and mameys. At the side was a porcelain soup tureen.

"It's Cristy and Joaquín," the woman said, smiling even more. The man picked up the napkin from his lap and dropped it on the table. He got up and went over to Cristina. Alicia explained, she left home with her little brother. I told her you and Mamá promised not to tell her parents. She's my best friend, Papá. The man squatted down and looked at Cristina over his horn-rimmed glasses with that cold, unchanging look.

"Now, Cristy, tell me what happened."

"Well . . . once Alicia told me she could lend me some money if I needed it . . ."

"But what was it that happened? Why did you leave home?"

Cristina looked down at the scuffed tips of her shoes.

"I woke up in the morning and . . . my parents weren't there. They went away."

"They're coming back, Cristy."

"Yes, but it's not that . . ."

"Do they scold you very much?"

"No, they're very nice."

"Then?"

"They yell."

"That's all? All the parents in the world do that, Cristy."

"At night?"

"Yes, at night. And sometimes during the day. It's normal."

"You promised not to tell them."

"Of course we did. We promised . . . Have you and Joaquín eaten?"

"No." Cristina kept her gaze trained on the tips of her shoes and crossed her hands behind her back.

"Come," the woman said, leading them to the table. The cat was on the patio drinking some milk.

"I have to peepee," the child said looking at his sister almost as soon as they were seated.

"I'll take him," the woman said, indicating Cristina should stay seated. But the child turned trembling lips toward her:

"Keetee."

She got up and, guided by the servant, took her brother to the bathroom. When they got back, there were two steaming bowls of soup for them. They ate it in silence. Cristina answered the woman's questions in monosyllables. What do your parents talk about? And how late? Didn't they leave you a note? Does your mother cry a lot? Does your father yell at her? But the man only watched them very closely as he cut pieces of meat and put them

17

in his mouth to chew slowly, pushing out his jaw. Seeing him there, so serious, at the head of the table, Cristina was reminded of her father and had trouble swallowing her food. If she could have run away . . . When they finished dessert—ice cream with a slice of mamey—the man told them to go play on the patio, Alicia had some beautiful skates.

"We need to go," Cristina said.

"For a while. Then you can go," as if it were an order.

It was no use trying to leave at that moment. Better to pretend to play happily and find a way to escape later. But first Cristina looked steadily at the man, stood up, and confirmed what she already knew, what she suddenly knew to be already inside her (even though that particular morning, it was different), a kind of morbidness, a pleasure in what could only increase the pain of the decision.

"Do you really promise?" she asked, standing in front of him, biting her lip while waiting for the answer.

"Of course," he said more with his lips than with his cold eyes, pinching the girl's cheek.

He's lying, Cristina told herself, and he knows I know he's lying.

For several delightful hours Cristina felt a strange happiness that she hadn't experienced for a long time. Perhaps since the vacation she spent with her grandmother—the two of them alone for two weeks in the big house in Puebla.

They skated around the patio fountain while Joaquín amused himself with Lucas and made triangles and cubes out of building blocks. Then they played with puppets in Alicia's bedroom. She kept suggesting one game after another, tirelessly, and Cristina responded, waving her hands and dancing around. It all brought on a special feeling when she remembered the events of the morning. The columns in the hall provided ideal hiding places, and they could also hide in the dining room or on the patio. They ran from one place to another, shrieking whenever they found each other. And during one of those moments Cristina seized the chance to escape. Alicia's mother had invited them to spend the night (nobody will know, trust us), and Cristina pretended to accept with a smile. Now they wouldn't see the lady again. Everything seemed calm when Cristina grabbed Joaquín's hand and ran with him to the door. Alicia was coming behind them:

"They promised!"

The boy sobbed because Lucas had stayed behind, but Cristina thought only of the door to the street (and what if they had locked it with a key so they couldn't get out?).

6 **With Joaquín crying constantly for Lucas,** she didn't stop until they reached Insurgentes. A motorcycle almost ran into them crossing the avenue. All thoughts and images had fled: Cristina felt her body was being pushed by a strange, independent force, something that seemed to surge up from the earth, from far below the earth, or from the cold wind that burned in her chest.

"You're mean!" Joaquín said to her. "I hope you die!" and then, in a voice full of pleading, "Let's go get Lucas!"

But Cristina was more concerned about the coats, which she had also been unable to rescue.

Joaquín seemed to calm down briefly as he breathed in big gulps of air, but as soon as he looked up at the sky—as if his cat were there—he began again, even louder.

"You're bad!"

"We can't go back for Lucas. You have to understand that," and Cristina held the bag tighter against her side.

When his sobbing seemed to engulf the child, she said,

"Alicia will take care of him. And some day we'll go back for him, I promise you."

They took the first bus that passed by. It didn't matter to Cristina where it went, as long as she got as far away as possible from that house. They were exhausted. As soon as they got seats, Joaquín fell asleep, and soon she did, too.

She dreamed she was still in Alicia's house, playing hide-and-seek. Only in the dream, the thing she feared happened. Coming out of a bedroom, she bumped into the overwhelming, brutal presence of Papá, who smiled at her and opened his arms. Cristina felt something break inside her and screamed. As if continuing the game, she ran down the hall and into a corner to hide. In her dream, the time she stayed there, curled up, trembling and holding back a sob, seemed interminable. But Papá was already coming down the hall, calling her, Cristy, my little girl, and behind him came Alicia's parents and Mamá, who was carrying Joaquín, and she knew her cries of I don't want to, I don't want to, no, were useless because Papá knew how to control her, carry her, press her against him, hold her legs with one hand and make her strength slip away little by little.

She woke up and felt happy to realize her freedom. But how long would it last? She imagined Papá notifying all the police patrols, all the radio stations. Once she had heard them looking for runaway children on the radio. "They left their house this morning . . . You will receive a reward . . . If you have any information, call telephone numbers . . ." Would they be able to escape? It was so easy to identify them—a ten-year-old girl with a four-year-old boy. From that moment on, she felt a thousand eyes watching them. She started to pray "Our Father, who art in Heaven" to ask Him to help her, but stopped. It amused her to look out the window and see faces disappearing, being left behind as if they'd never existed. She calmed down—Joaquín was sleeping peacefully, and it was a beautiful afternoon with a brilliant sky. Where could they get the out-of-town buses and trains? And would the three hundred pesos in her purse be enough? She thought about asking the driver, but was terrified by the idea that he would suspect something and call the police, or take them to the police station himself. With strangers you never know.

When they entered a neighborhood with taco stands and gray houses, as if the sun had suddenly darkened, she became fearful and thought it would be better to get off and take another bus. It was difficult to awaken Joaquín, who insisted on going back for Lucas and cried for Mamá.

"You have to understand, Joaquín!" she told him in a sharp voice, shaking him by his shoulders.

Joaquín seemed to realize the gravity of the situation because he became very serious and let her pull him along. They got off in a crowded street of houses with paint peeling off the walls and shops surrounded by clouds of smoke heavy with the odor of barbecue. Hungry dogs with begging eyes roamed the area. Cristina held Joaquín's hand tightly as they walked around the block on the edge of the sidewalk. A fat, dark man leaning against a wall followed them with a look that was like a searchlight. Cristina felt an overwhelming urge to run, but felt sure that if she attracted his attention, he would catch up with them very quickly.

"Walk straight ahead, Joaquín. Don't turn around."

"Why?"

And the first thing the child did was turn around. Cristina dug her fingernails into her palms.

"A policeman might come, Joaquín."

It frightened the child. Cristina was obsessed with the police. She looked for them everywhere, fantasized seeing them come around the corner or out of the next doorway, like in those haunted houses when just as when you fear it most, a hand comes up to wring your neck. So she preferred walking slowly. She turned after a moment to be sure the man by the fence was no longer watching them. She felt a sea of eyes watching her.

At the corner she stopped to ask where the international bus station was and how much a ticket would cost. After asking the question, she noticed the fixed expression of the man in front of her, like on a wax figure.

"Huh?"

For a minute they kept looking at each other in silence, the man swaying and Cristina fearing he would fall on her with all his weight.

Cristina and Joaquín were moving away, but the man followed them a few steps and even put his hand out toward them. To Cristina it seemed like the hand in her fantasy.

"Wait, little girl . . ."

Her resistance gave way to uncontrollable fear, and Cristina ran as hard as she could, making Joaquín fall. He started to cry again. They reached the end of the block and stopped before turning. Cristina had a pain in her side and Joaquín shrieked:

"Mamá!"

"Be quiet, Joaquín, or I'm going to hit you!"

"I don't want to run! I want to go home!"

"We're not going home. We're never going home! Understand? You're always going to live with me. I'll be with you always."

From the child's lips came a bubble that seemed to contain a strangled cry.

7 **They walked toward a small park** with bare trees and dry earth. A group of dark children were playing soccer with a flabby ball that hardly budged. The dust made Cristina's eyes burn. Joaquín seemed to feel better when he saw the game, and he even dropped his sister's hand. The sun was setting in the distance.

Cristina saw a church at the end of the park, and her heart lightened. Maybe they could spend the night there. Also, its mere existence comforted her. She looked at the high belfry outlined against the afternoon and remembered the words of Father Roldán, an old friend of the family: "Only praying and being close to God will save us. All the rest is Hell." And Cristina opened her eyes wide, "Hell? With fire?" The priest smiled and patted her cheek. "Yes, with a big fire, though we won't see it." Mamá protested: "Father, what kind of things are you telling her?" The priest sat her on his lap: "So she'll know and begin to recognize the place she's fallen to." And Cristina's mind was engraved with the image of the flames we do not see and the invisible fire that surrounds us. At times, even when she was happiest, she thought she could see high, rose-colored tongues around her, feel their heat, and imagine their quivering shadows making designs on the wall.

There were very few people around. All she could hear was the low murmur of a group of women in dark shawls saying their rosaries in the front pews. Cristina passed by one woman who glanced at her out of the corner of her eye, bent over, and hid her rosary even more in her hands, as if the girl might attack her or rob her. Cristina and Joaquín sat down in a pew; she held his hand very tightly and began to look around. A saint looked down on her from the top of a column with a chiding gesture and pointing a finger on high as if signaling her guilt: "Ah, Cristina, ah!" Cristina shivered. Was this the place where she was going to feel calmer? In a stained glass window, where a bright yellow light filtered through, the Virgin Mary was holding the Christ Child in her lap with nebulous hands that seemed to rock him without moving him while she looked at him with half-closed eyes. Cristina concentrated on that window and, although she tried not to, remembered when she used to go to sleep in her mother's arms. She was sure the image—curiously similar to the one in the window—had been real some years earlier. Mamá had cuddled her, telling her to go to sleep, that nothing was going to happen, that she was there to take care of her and so was Papá. Joaquín was not yet born, and she felt she could abandon herself in her mother's arms without having to think of anything, simply close her eyes and be in another place where there were no conflicts, nor yelling, nor fire. She did not remember the feeling exactly, but was sure it was as she imagined.

However, something had changed that night when she awakened crying out because she dreamed Papá was burning in the flames. Mamá had come to her bedroom and had told her nothing had happened to Papá, he was sleeping very quietly, and she should do the same, and all three of them would always be very happy, and so would the expected little brother. And Mamá had tucked her in and blessed her, saying, my beautiful little girl, my princess, my little sweetness. That night—how long ago was it?—she did not believe that really nothing would happen to them, and the following day she moved around like a sleepwalker, not concentrating on anything. There seemed to be a presence, a shadow, hovering over her and Mamá and Papá, something indefinable that would happen soon.

Joaquín remained asleep in her lap as she stroked his hair. In spite of everything, she felt happy to be there with Joaquín. It would be good if they could spend the night in the church and tomorrow find out how to get out of the city . . . She leaned back in the pew.

She was awakened by the sharp voice of a priest with white hair and dark eyebrows who was bending over them and looking at them furiously.

"Hey, hey, what are you doing here . . . We're going to close up the church. You have to leave."

"Couldn't we . . . ?"

"Come on. You have to leave. What are you doing here at this hour?"

"But, just tonight . . ."

"Tonight, what?"

"To sleep here, my little brother and me."

"Are you crazy? Don't you have a home?"

"Yes, we do, but . . . just tonight."

"What? I've already told you we have to close the church."

The priest seemed to be really anxious, opening and closing his hands as if he were squeezing lemons.

"Where are your parents?" he insisted.

"Well, they're not here because . . . they've gone on a trip. But if we can stay here, an aunt is coming tomorrow to get us . . ."

"Aunt or no aunt. Do you live near here?"

"Yes."

"Then go home, go on." And he grabbed her arm pulling her up.

"Joaquín, Joaquín!" Cristina said, trying to wake him, but he was sound asleep.

"Come on, come on, child!" and he almost made her fall.

"Joaquín!"

The boy woke up crying.

"We have to go, Joaquín."

The child stood up, still crying, and his sister pulled him by the hand toward the big wooden door, followed closely by the priest, walking bent over and waving his arms to hurry them.

As she went out, Cristina turned to say please, but stopped when she saw those eyes in the silvery light from the street. They were eyes such as she had never seen, with a glare of cast iron. And then the half-open mouth, as if about to drool. She took two steps back and grabbed Joaquín's hand.

"All right, we're going."

But the priest didn't hear her because he went back into the church and Cristina heard the screech of the key in the lock. And then another key in the lock below, with turn after turn that seemed to harden the wood.

8 **Cristina looked bleakly** at the night spreading over the park, deepening it, turning it into a well. Farther on, there were still lights and noise. They crossed the street and went to sit on a bench. It's so hard, Cristina thought, feeling the cold cement on her thighs. Joaquín began crying.

"I want my mamá."

"Go back to sleep."

"I'm hungry."

They crossed the park and came out on a run-down street Cristina had not been on before. She turned and looked all around her and tried to remember which street the bus had left them on and which one they had taken to the park, but could not do it. It was strange. She felt lost, but the feeling stimulated her. There were dimly lighted shops on the street with small groups of men outside talking loudly, excitedly. She walked very close to the wall, with her arm around Joaquín, to the next corner, where they found a cart with roasted ears of corn. She asked for two and the woman attending it removed the metal sheet that served as a lid. A burst of steam escaped, and the woman asked if they wanted them with chile.

"One with a little and the other without, please. And a lot of lemon."

Cristina held out a hundred-peso bill, took the ears of corn by the sticks at each end, and asked Joaquín to take the change.

"Put it in my purse."

In trying to open the purse, the child dropped the bills and the coins.

"Oh, what a boy."

Cristina had to put the ears down on the cart near the bottle of chile piquín to pick up the bills and look for the coins. Seven pesos were missing. The woman looked at them indifferently.

"Help me, Joaquín!"

But the child tried to reach one of the ears and almost knocked over the bottle of chile piquín. The woman screamed and managed to rescue the teetering bottle.

"Joaquín!" his sister yelled at him.

"I want my corn."

"Get away from here, you little brats!" and she shook a huge hand in front of Cristina's face.

Cristina put in her purse the money she had retrieved from the ground without separating it, the bills rolled in a ball, then picked up the corn and told her brother to follow her because she could not hold his hand. The boy went down the dark street behind her. Before they got to the first group of men talking in front of a cantina or taco stand—she could not tell which it was—she told Joaquín to hold on to her dress.

The men turned to look at them and she tried to look natural, smiling at them. But her smile was a frigid, terrified grimace as one of the men, with a beer bottle in his hand, yelled "Boo!" at them and then burst out laughing. Cristina walked faster and told her brother to hold her dress tighter.

Reaching the park, she made sure no one was following them and looked for the bench in the best light, although darkness was deepening in the whole park.

"You see, you made us lose seven pesos, you dummy," she said to her brother as they ate the ears of corn.

"I want some milk."

"We don't have any milk. You'll have to wait."

Joaquín only nibbled at the corn, and with the child's promise that he would eat it the next day, Cristina wrapped it in her handkerchief and put it in her purse.

Then she saw a bent, humpbacked woman coming near, leaning on a piece of broomstick. She wore a dress of frayed black netting. Cristina had no time to react, so she kept still, holding her breath and hugging her brother.

"What are you two doing here?"

"Well . . . we were going to sleep."

"To sleep here?"

"Yes, here . . . Or can't we?"

"Yes, you can. Of course you can. But don't you have a home?"

"Yes, but we ran away." It was as though fear made her tell the truth.

The woman came closer to look at them, turning her head to one side as if looking through a magnifying glass. She had watery, bulging eyes and waxy skin tightly drawn over her bones. In her dirty white hair that came down to her shoulders there were wilted flowers, some almost all stem.

"And why did you run away? Tell me."

"Because . . . we wanted to."

The woman came a little closer and her breath made Cristina throw back her head, resting it on the back of the bench.

"So you just wanted to, huh?"

"Well, yes."

"Your brother also wanted to?" and she looked at Joaquín, who turned shy and hid his head behind his sister's shoulder.

"No, he didn't want to, but later he will."

"How come you're so sure?"

"Because I know."

"Did your parents beat you much?"

"No, they never beat us."

"Then, what's the problem?"

"Sometimes . . . they yelled."

"Was that all?"

"Yes."

The woman laughed loudly, exposing shriveled, pale pink gums. "Stupid brat."

Another loud laugh. She shivered as if she had a fever. Some withered flowers fell off her head like off a tree being shaken.

"So you're going to support this little boy?"

"Yes, I'm going to look for a job."

"How old are you?"

Cristina's cheeks reddened.

"Ten . . . but I'm going on eleven," she said, looking down.

"If I were ten and had parents like yours, do you know what I would do?" and she came closer again, holding her head on one side, as if she saw only with one eye. "I'd lie in my bed with a cat, eating chocolates. Do you like cats?"

Joaquín's eyes lighted up when he heard the word *cat*.

"My brother adores them," Cristina explained. "He lost his."

"I love cats," the woman said, holding out a bony hand toward Joaquín. "I take all the cats I find to my house. Wouldn't you like to sleep with a cat, child?"

Joaquín nodded his head, opening his eyes even wider.

Cristina was afraid, but let herself be guided through the vacant streets. Anyway, any place was better than a bench in the park. The night was clear and blue with a moon like a streetlight that made tall shadows: a woman bent over her broomstick and Cristina and Joaquín hand in hand.

9 **The woman stopped** at some piles of garbage to look for food.

"You can always find something here," she said.

Next to the metal door of what appeared to be a taco stand, she drove off a dog with her stick and found some bits of meat among greasy papers and empty beer bottles. Cristina felt nausea when she saw her chew on a bone until it was clean.

"Do you want some?" she asked, holding it up and smiling at them.

Cristina shook her head and moved her brother a little farther away.

"Have you already had supper?"

Cristina explained they had bought some ears of corn and almost a whole one was left over for Joaquín's breakfast. The woman left the garbage and wanted to see it. Cristina took it out of her purse and held it up without removing the handkerchief, but the woman grabbed it, threw the handkerchief on the ground, and began to eat it avidly.

"Hey, that's my brother's."

"Bah, we'll get something else tomorrow."

Cristina resigned herself. There was nothing else to do. She added the cost of the corn to the lost pesos and decided not to say anything to the woman about the money she was carrying. She kept on walking.

"What kind of job do you have?"

"I don't need one," the woman said. "From time to time some money falls into this little pouch," as she pointed to the bulky pocket of her dress. "But in this lousy neighborhood everybody knows me, and they don't want to give me anything. Also, they're poor. So I go to the rich neighborhoods. I spend a while in one and when they get tired of me, I look for another. Although some days I don't get enough for the bus and have to walk back."

Joaquín was falling asleep and held up his arms to ask his sister to carry him. But with only a hard look from her, he resigned himself and even walked faster, very serious. Cristina was astonished.

"Is it much farther, Señora?"

"No, we're almost there. And don't call me Señora . . . I hate Señoras. Call me Angustias."

They entered a narrow, dark alley with damp stains on the walls and overflowing garbage cans.

"No point in looking in them. There's never anything worth the trouble."

They crossed a patio with laundry tubs and clothes hung to dry. A man seated in a rocking chair that creaked showed them two uneven, yellow teeth in greeting.

"In a little while, right?"

"Yes, Jesús," she said without even turning.

The man lifted a bottle from the ground and held it up proudly to show her.

"Want some?"

"Not today."

"And those children?"

"They're my little friends."

"You're not going to . . ." and he laughed out loud and threw his body back. The rocking chair gave a sharp shriek, like a lament.

The woman pushed aside the clothes with her broomstick.

"What a nuisance. How many times have I told them not to hang clothes here. That's what the roof is for."

The doors were metal, and the small windows had flowered curtains that gave off a dull light.

At the end of the patio, Angustias stopped in front of a door and looked for the key in the pocket of her dress.

"This is my humble abode."

She opened the door and, before entering, struck a match.

"We haven't had electricity for years."

Cristina heard the meowing and felt a cramp in her stomach.

"I don't want to go in," Joaquín said.

"They're cats, Joaquín."

But her tone of voice betrayed her. The door to the room looked more like the mouth of a dark cave.

Angustias had lighted the candle on the table, and it seemed to Cristina that the eyes of the cats were gleaming even more.

"Stop that! Stop that!" Angustias said, hitting them with the stick. "You're all over each other."

She threw them some pieces of meat.

"Eat, eat . . . you devilish cats."

She was stepping on their tails, thrusting her stick in their mouths and grabbing the meat she had just given them, while they meowed furiously all around her, like in a circus act.

"Cats from hell . . ."

She looked at Cristina and, with a smile darkened by the flickering light of the candle, said, "They're like my children."

Joaquín pressed himself against his sister, hanging onto her dress with both hands, and said, "I want to go."

"They're cats, Joaquín. Don't you like them as much?"

"They're not Lucas," he said, pointing to them.

"All cats are alike, Joaquín."

"Sit down," the woman said, indicating one of the two chairs at the table. "Or you can go to bed now if you want to."

Things seemed to float in the twilight—the bed of rusty metal, with a wool spread so torn it looked as if it would come apart; the worm-eaten dresser with a small lace cover on it; a candlestick; and an oval picture of a smiling old woman who was holding her head as if she wanted to come out of the picture.

"This furniture is the only thing I have left from my mother; all the rest is gone . . . ," Angustias explained in a sad voice with a tone of farewell, as she sat at the table in front of the candle, which made her expression even more enigmatic. "Look, child, that's her."

Cristina went close to look at the photograph and said, "How beautiful." She felt a sad tenderness in her stomach. The only thing she had left from her mother. Cristina had nothing left from her mother. And she would never go back home, so she would never have a memento of her mother. She would like to have had something. A rosary, for instance. Her mother had a collection of rosaries which she hung behind the door of her bedroom. At that moment—there in the dimness produced by the candle—she would like to have had something that belonged to her mother, anything, to hold tightly.

"I used to have pictures," the woman said, "but I sold them. Or they disappeared . . . and I had a bureau, but it's gone, too."

"I'm afraid," Joaquín said.

"Calm down, Joaquín."

"I have to peepee."

"Señora," Cristina asked very seriously, "may I use your bathroom?"

"Of course, of course," and she indicated the door.

"May I take the candle?"

Three cats followed Cristina, meowing and rubbing against her legs. She thought, I can't bear this, but then told herself she had to bear it and tried to think of something else. In the corner next to the bathroom door, there were empty cans and bottles, papers, and dry branches.

"I don't need to peepee," Joaquín said when he looked into the bathroom.

"Come on, Joaquín, or you'll do it during the night," and she made him go in.

The first thing Cristina noticed was the absence of a shower. She thought, how awful, where does she bathe? There was only a dirty wash basin, a medicine cabinet with a broken mirror, and a toilet without a lid. She put the saucer with the candle on the basin and, looking up, caught part of her reflection in the mirror. She turned her head to see the rest of her face and felt dizzy. She blinked. What am I doing here, so alone, and with my brother?

Joaquín tugged on her skirt.

"I'm doing it."

She pushed down his pants and underwear and seated him on the toilet.

"I have to go poopoo, too."

Cristina looked for some toilet paper, but could not find any. She went out to ask the woman, though she could only see her silhouette.

"There are some newspapers over there," she said, pointing to the corner. Cristina went to get the candle and Joaquín shrieked.

"It's dark!"

"Wait, honey."

The cats followed her, making her more nervous. She looked for the newspaper that was least dirty. The woman remained motionless in the chair, her aquiline profile silhouetted against the subdued light that came through the bare window. Joaquín was sobbing loudly in the bathroom.

"I'm coming, Joaquín, I'm coming."

She tore off a piece of paper to clean the child. Then she pulled up his underwear and pants and they left the bathroom. Now the woman was seated with her chin resting on her chest, and Cristina supposed she was asleep. She put the candle beside her, saying "Thank you."

The cats were walking all around, and Joaquín held up his hand so they could not lick it.

"Señora, where are we going to sleep?"

"Huh?" said the woman, shaking her head so that some wilted flowers fell on the table. "Ah, my little precious, my beautiful little cubs," and she held out her hand to stroke Joaquín's cheek, "I'm going to be like your Mamá, you'll see, I'm going to take care of you, keep you in my heart. Come, come."

Cristina felt sick to her stomach when the woman pulled her over to embrace her and kiss her hair.

"Would you like to sleep with me? Come, we'll sleep together, all of us together, my little kittens, you and me."

She stood up, went to the bed, and lifted the bedspread.

"Come on, get in here."

Cristina took off Joaquín's sweater and shoes and put them with hers at the bottom of the bed (she thought that if she put them on the floor, the cats would eat them). When she got in under the bedspread, she felt the mattress spring in her back. Her purse hurt her side, but she didn't dare take it off.

When the woman got in bed and the cats got on top, she felt the urge to jump up and run to call her mother on the phone. But she thought anything was preferable, less painful, than going back to the same thing as all those nights past. Closing her eyes, she clenched her teeth. Joaquín fell asleep immediately, but Cristina had a cat right on top of her chest, and the woman embraced her, closing in with her fetid breath.

I need to pray, she told herself.

Then she clenched her teeth even tighter, and felt two large tears roll down her cheeks.

10 **Cristina dreamed** about the house in the country where they had spent vacations when Joaquín was a little baby and for her the world had consisted of Papá and Mamá. But in the dream, she was her real age, and so was Joaquín. She and her brother tiptoed down the stairs, unlocked the door and opened it very slowly to lessen its creak. They went out into a cloudy, windy night. Going around the house, they went to the window of the small room where their parents were sitting in front of the fireplace. He was reading, and she sat with her eyes half-closed, moving back and forth in a rocking chair. The fire was casting shadows and surrounding them with a yellow glow. Papá was so still he looked like a wax figure. Cristina stuck her face against the glass, as if she wanted to get to the other side, and felt very sad. She was going to call to them, but only moved her lips against the glass as if she were kissing it. Joaquín tugged on her dress the way he always did and asked her to pick him up so he could see Papá and Mamá, too, but Cristina turned with a finger to her lips and said, Let's go.

They walked through a forest of pine trees swaying in the wind. The sky was burning with streaks of blue lightning. Cristina preferred the darkness to the rays of light, which lit up the animals stampeding, the pines piercing the sky, the eyes of the owls.

They tried to cross the river on the smooth rocks, but Joaquín slipped and fell into the water. Cristina held out her hand to him, but the child was slowly sinking, waving his arms and crying out to his sister. She grabbed his arm and pulled him, but without much strength because she was slipping on the rocks and about to fall.

The water was up to his neck; he was no longer churning it, and yet, she could tell only by the movements of his lips, he was still calling her, and calling Mamá, with his eyes open wider than she had ever seen them.

Then Cristina saw him sink, illuminated by a flash of lightning, and with it the rain began: raindrops making small, concentric circles in the water. She screamed and put her hands over her eyes. She felt the rain on her cheeks but, suddenly awake, discovered it was tears and rubbed them away with the back of her hand. The woman was sleeping on her back, snoring loudly with a sharp whistle. On the other side of the bed, Joaquín was sleeping with his face to the wall. Cristina tried to dislodge the cat that was sleeping on her chest, but when awakened, it meowed and started to scratch her, so she decided to leave it alone. She had never imagined she could sleep with a cat on her, since she disliked them so much (even Lucas). She hugged her brother, feeling happy it had only been a dream, and also happy to be spending the night so far from home.

11 **The creaking of the door** awakened her. When Cristina sat up, the cat on her chest jumped to the floor. In the open door she saw the silhouette of a man. Cristina rubbed her eyes. Was she dreaming again? The man was still there, like an apparition, as if certain that only he could see clearly. Cristina gripped the edge of the bedspread and said, "Papá?"

But the man did not answer.

The woman continued sleeping on her back, and Joaquín, with his face to the wall. Then the man took a few steps forward, and Cristina noticed that he was staggering. He went to the bed and leaned over her, as if he were going to fall on his face. She shrieked when she saw a gleam, like lightning, in his eyes.

"What's going on?" the woman said, sitting up and looking around.

"Angustias," the man said.

The woman showed her yellow teeth in what might have been either a smile or a gesture of disgust. Cristina pressed up against her brother. The woman held out her arms.

"Jesús, come to bed with us."

The man leaned over the bed a little more and half-opened his thick mouth, showing two teeth in his upper gum. His eyes shone brighter.

"Angustias."

He came up to the head of the bed, and the light coming through the window fell directly on his face. Then Cristina recognized the man she had seen when she entered the alley.

"Come, Jesús, come."

He's drunk, Cristina thought, and remembered the only time she saw Papá with eyes like that. He had returned from a party and came to give her a kiss, as always, before going to bed. She hardly woke up, but at breakfast the next morning, she said to her mother:

"Papá was drunk last night."

"My dear," Mamá said without lifting her face from her plate.

The man sat on the edge of the bed. He stretched out a hand that made Cristina pull back more, and caressed the woman's head.

"Your flowers," he said. "Flowers in your hair."

"Come, come to bed."

"Who are those children?"

"Some little friends I found in the park. Poor things, they don't want to go back home. They hate their parents."

Cristina was going to make it clear that she didn't hate her parents, but she didn't dare. The woman caressed her forehead.

"Go to sleep, my love."

And she turned around to the man.

"You're really drunk."

"Angustias," he said again.

"I'll make a little space for you. Come," and she lifted the spread. The man got in bed next to her, and Cristina felt the weight of them both fall on her. The cats, who had been walking around the man's legs, returned to the bed, and one, undoubtedly the same one, got on top of Cristina.

"My Jesús."

"Wow, you can't imagine how drunk."

"Put your hand here. Like that. Mmh, farther down. How wonderful."

"You're hot, Angustias."

"Very."

"Those damned kids are going to see us."

"They're asleep. Come on."

The man uncovered the woman's flabby breasts, and Cristina looked more closely, with a curiosity that diminished her fear.

"Like this?"

He got on top of the woman under the spread, and they made a high, dark wave. The woman moaned, and the man appeared to be drowning. They're making love, Cristina thought, and remembered seeing something similar in a movie. She was amused by it, even leaning her head on the palm of her hand.

For a little while the wave rose so much and the man had so much trouble breathing, it seemed he was about to explode. On the other hand, the woman's face sank into the pillow as if it were foam, and her expression of being about to bite something, to pull it up by the roots, had changed into an ecstatic, frozen grin that made Cristina think of pain.

But she was entertained and even had to smother a laugh with the back of her hand when the man shook as if he had received an electric charge, sucked in as much air as he possibly could and then fell on the woman, sinking into her bosom while she asked for more, my Jesús, more, crying out so loudly Cristina was afraid she would waken Joaquín.

Cristina remembered the morning when Alicia told her, I saw

my parents do that thing they call making love. Love? That's what they call it. They came together and got on top of each other in bed. I didn't see it very well, but I saw it more or less. They came together? Cristina asked, pretending to know what it was about. Yes, very close together, Alicia told her.

And in a movie, when a couple went into a bedroom and were kissing and slowly falling on the bed and the light went out to change the scene, she turned to her mother and asked,

"They came together?"

And her mother answered her with a finger to her lips, saying, "My dear."

Cristina would have liked to see them again, in more detail, but the man immediately fell asleep on the woman's bare breast, as peaceful as a child, and the woman stroked his hair for a while, saying, my little Jesús, and suddenly dropped her hand, letting it fall as if she had no strength. She started that snoring of hers, which was more like whistling.

Cristina thought, if I could only get this cat off me, but she didn't even try, and a few moments later she, too, was asleep.

12 **When Cristina awakened,** with the sun slanting through the window, Joaquín was no longer at her side. Her hand was resting in the hollow the child had left in the pillow. She looked at it as if trying to focus on it, recognize it, not really sure it was her normal, everyday hand, and suddenly, remembering everything, reacted to the absence of her brother.

"Joaquín," she said, sitting up and looking all around.

Angustias, who was seated at the table taking small sips from a mug, answered without looking at her.

"He went with Jesús."

"Where?"

The light was revealing things, stripping them of the halo of the night before: the rust on the metal bed, the threadbare bedspread, the stains on the mattress, the springs sticking through, the cat dung on the floor, the pile of newspapers in one corner, the damp stains on the walls, the layer of dust that covered everything. Terror dawned in Cristina's eyes.

"I want to see my brother."

"You'll see him this afternoon, after we get back from work."

"No!"

Cristina jumped on Angustias, and the cats meowed. The contents of the mug—something that looked like coffee with milk—spilled on the table. Cristina grabbed Angustias by both shoulders and in return received a blow in the mouth from the back of her hand.

"Just look what you've done, you stupid brat," Angustias said, picking up the mug and using a spoon to try to catch the liquid that was spreading across the top of the table. But Cristina came back with even more fury and seized Angustias' hair.

"I want to see my brother!" she shouted again.

Angustias gave a long moan and arched her back, letting the spoon fall. But a single jab of her elbow in the girl's stomach was enough to make her release the hair. Then she turned with enraged eyes and slapped her several times on her head and face. Cristina still managed to respond with a kick, but one blow made her fall to the floor, where she put her hands up to her mouth and nose, both bleeding profusely.

She was crying as she screamed, "Joaquín!"

"Be quiet or I'll hit you again! You'll have all the neighbors in here!"

The cats circled around them, their eyes infected with excitement.

Cristina stopped crying and begged:

"I want to see my little brother."

"I've already told you that you'll see him this afternoon."

"If you don't let me see him, I'll scream until all the neighbors come."

"Before you do that, I'll break your teeth and cut out your tongue to make you stop screaming."

Cristina was terrified by the possibility of losing her tongue. Angustias guessed it, because she repeated it, adding another threat.

"I'll cut your tongue into bits and then cut out your brother's."

"Joaquín is just a little boy!"

"Shut up! You're going to do what I tell you. You'll go to work with me, and when we get back, you'll see him."

"Who will take care of him?"

"Jesús."

"Well, let me see him just once before we go."

"Come," and she held out a hand. "Wipe off your face with the bedspread."

Cristina obeyed. Then they went to a room two doors away and Angustias told her to go to the window, but not to let her brother see her, so he would not make a fuss. Cristina saw Joaquín's back. He was seated on the bed, playing with some paper figures Jesús was cutting out for him with a pair of large scissors. She was going to call him, but Angustias repeated the threat in her ear.

"Remember, I'll cut out your tongue."

Angustias took her by the arm and pushed her toward the street.

"If you say anything, anything at all, I'll go cut out your brother's tongue right now."

A woman who was hanging up clothes said to Cristina,

"Don't go with that crazy old woman, child," and then, when she saw her closer, "What happened to your face?"

"I fell," Cristina said, feeling the pressure of Angustias' fingers on her arm.

By the time they got to the street, Cristina realized how much her nose and mouth were hurting.

13 **Cristina burst out crying.** Angustias stopped her at a corner and squatted down so she could talk to her looking into her eyes, as she moved her forefinger and middle finger back and forth like scissors.

"You're going to be quiet, because if you're not, look."

Cristina blinked, seeing the movement of her fingers.

"Show me your tongue."

"No!" She was going to run, but the woman grabbed her with a hand that to Cristina felt like pliers on her arm.

"So you're going to behave now, aren't you?"

Trembling, she nodded her head and looked at the ground. A drop of blood from the corner of her mouth made a red stain on her dress, like a confirmation of her fear.

"Now you're going to take my hand and go where I tell you to, without crying or talking."

Cristina obeyed. They walked two blocks, Cristina never raising her eyes.

"Do you have any money in that purse?" the woman asked her.

"No."

"Let me see."

"I have a hundred pesos."

"Give them to me."

Cristina clutched the purse to her chest with both hands, as if she were protecting her heart.

"They're to buy food for my little brother."

"Give them to me, or I'll take them from you."

Cristina slipped her fingers in the purse like tweezers. She gave the hundred-peso bill to the woman and closed the purse nervously. Angustias showed her gums in laughter.

"Stupid brat. I know you have more money."

Cristina withdrew again, staring at the ground, and muttered between her teeth, "I hate her!"

They took a bus to a residential neighborhood and got off at a wide street with poplar trees. They walked down the street.

"Look, that's the church I usually stand outside," she said, pointing to a cross that seemed to float above the tops of the trees, "but today we're going to do another little job."

She took her to a house that looked like a castle with parapets, a fountain in the garden, and bare trees. They sat on the wall at the base of the high grillwork and the woman took a small jug out of her pocket, put two coins in it, and made them jingle whenever someone passed by—which was only sporadically. A woman pushing a fat, rosy baby in a carriage dropped three pennies in the jug and smiled at Cristina.

"And this little girl?"

"She's my little granddaughter. So sweet, she's keeping me company," Angustias said.

"Is she your grandmother?"

Cristina nodded her head.

"What happened to your mouth?"

"I fell."

"Do you live nearby?"

Cristina nodded again.

"What a pretty baby," Angustias said, bending over to caress him, but the woman avoided that by pushing the carriage ahead. Then she left, with another smile.

"You did very well," Angustias said to Cristina. "There are very few people on this street, but you have to be careful anyway. I brought you here so you can help me get into one of the houses."

"Which one?"

"This one," Angustias answered, looking out of the corner of her eye at the house behind them. "You can go in between the railings."

"And if they see me?" and she touched the rusty metal and looked fearfully at the sharp arrows on top.

"They're not going to see you. When I tell you, you'll stand on this base, squeeze into the garden, and enter the house through the kitchen door. On a shelf above the stove there are some keys. Bring all of them."

"Right now?" and Cristina looked at the parapets of the house as if at any moment someone might appear there.

"I'll tell you when."

Cristina sat back down on the wall while the woman cut some flowers off the shrubs in the street and put them in her hair. Cristina leaned her head against the railing and closed her eyes.

As soon as she closed her eyes, the dream from the night before continued:

Papá, Mamá, Grandma, and she were on the bank of the river looking sadly at the place where Joaquín had gone under. The rain was covering the water with concentric circles. All four of them were watching, without moving.

"Here, here," Cristina was saying in a very low voice. In spite of the rain and the sound of the river, she knew Papá, Mamá, and Grandma were hearing her perfectly.

Again she awoke, happy it was only a dream. She longed more

than ever to see her brother, give him a big hug, and tell him she was going to take care of him forever and ever. However, even if she could escape, she wouldn't know how to find him. The woman was still walking around in the shrubs, cutting flowers. Her head was beginning to look like the designs Joaquín drew in school. It would have amused him a lot to see her, Cristina thought. Then, looking up at the sky, "Where are you, my little brother, where are you?" although she knew where he was and was sure nothing bad was happening to him. In a low voice, she said, "I'll be with you soon," while she clenched her teeth and frowned, as if sending a signal.

Angustias came back and gave her a flower, which Cristina put in her hair, too.

"My pretty little girl," Angustias said with eyes that had softened. "Precious."

14 **A woman came out** of the house, smiled at the old woman, and dropped a coin in the small jar.

Angustias watched her walk away and turn the corner, "Now," she said.

She made sure no one was coming and told Cristina to squeeze into the garden, go in through the kitchen door at the back of the house, find the key ring near the stove that she had told her about, and bring it quickly.

"How do you know about it?" Cristina asked, again beginning to feel fear in the pit of her stomach.

"I worked there for ten years."

Cristina ran through the garden, afraid of falling at every moment, imagining that the crackling of the dry leaves she was stepping on would betray her. And if a dog should come out? Or a man with a gun? They could take her to jail and from there notify her parents. She went past the stone fountain and walked slowly when she came to a narrow passageway—between a high wall covered with vines on one side and the side of the house on the other—which took her to the back patio, with its *pirul* trees and bare shrubs. She stayed close to the wall until she reached the screen door. What would happen if she opened it? Would there be a man waiting for her with a knife, ready to strike? And what was she doing there in that unfamiliar house? A terrifying image crossed her mind: that it was all a trick and her parents were inside (Papá with arms akimbo, and Mamá carrying Joaquín). She saw them outlined against the light without seeing their features . . . But that was absurd. They couldn't be there, and she had better make up her mind to go on in.

She took the key ring off the panel behind the stove and in a moment was back, dizzy and breathless, more from the fantasies than from the running. She passed the keys through the railing and waited for Angustias to enter. She had trouble with the keys, and Cristina kept jumping around and saying between her teeth, hurry, hurry up. She became even more uneasy when Angustias, as she entered the garden, stumbled on the edge of the tile walk that led to the main door, and Cristina had to help her get up and even hold her up because she was limping and, between moans, pointing to her beet-colored knee with its knotty veins so swollen they were about to burst.

In the house Angustias fell on a large couch covered with red silk and put her hurt knee and foot on the edge of the seat. As Cristina was walking around, very worried, someone would hear them, catch them, a policeman or Papá, and she almost knocked over a cut-glass flower bowl on a table in the middle of the room.

Angustias waved her bony hands over her injury and told Cristina to get some alcohol from the bathroom.

"They're going to put us in jail!"

"Be quiet, you wretched brat! The woman will be gone for a half hour, or longer if she's seeing her boyfriend. Go to the bathroom for some alcohol." She shook her fist.

"Where?" Angustias' threats immediately had the desired effect on the girl.

"Upstairs. Go look for it."

Cristina was looking at things as if she didn't believe them, as if she knew that when she remembered them, she wasn't going to believe them: the glass cabinet with small porcelain figures—why so many ducks?—the clock with a pendulum that was like a tired heart, the family pictures in gold frames, the tapestries on the stairs—whose house was it? And what were they going to steal? Before going up the last step, she stopped, stroked the handrail, and looked back at Angustias fussing over her injured knee; the windows with the curtains open so anyone passing on the street could see them . . . Her fear was like lead in her feet, keeping her from moving forward. Who was up there? There was no one who would defend her. She swallowed hard and began saying the Ave Maria. She went down a few steps to look into the dining room at the bronze fruit bowl with grapes, like a sun in the middle of the table.

Angustias suddenly appeared and yelled at her. "Bring the alcohol right now, you little fool!"

"I'm going to get some grapes. I haven't had any breakfast."

The look that hit her was enough to make her run upstairs.

But on the floor above, as she went near the first door, she heard a voice . . . A voice? She stopped with her legs rigid and a hand stretched out, like in a game of statues. Then there *was* someone. She dared to bend her neck closer and heard more clearly: "We-we-well . . . no-no-now . . ." It was a guttural, opaque voice, as if coming from someone speaking out of the depths of a cave.

She stumbled down the stairs, hardly able to talk by the time she reached Angustias.

"Someone . . . up there . . . I heard . . ."

Cristina could endure no more and started to cry. Angustias looked upstairs with an annoyed expression, but said mildly,

"All right, we'll go up together."

15 **Going up,** Cristina could not resist the desire to hold her hand, but since Angustias rejected her, she had to content herself with hanging onto her skirt. A Santa Teresa in a flowery frame looked at her with sympathetic eyes, as if caressing her.

"Poor Doña Luz," Angustias was telling her, "I know her very well. She's got time all mixed up. She thinks what happened yesterday is happening today and what's happening today happened yesterday. Her daughter committed suicide twenty years ago, and if you ask her, she'll say she has just seen her."

Angustias calmly opened the door where Cristina had heard the voice. The man with the knife held ready, the police, Papá . . .

"It's been so many years since I was in here," Angustias said.

Cristina held back, leaning against the doorway, and from there she saw the elderly lady in the brass bed, among lace pillowcases, wearing a cap and a shawl around her shoulders.

"Good evening, Doña Luz. It's Angustias," she said, sitting at the foot of the bed.

"Ah, Angustias." She opened her mouth so wide her jaw seemed to come loose and looked around with her eyes unfocused.

"Pretty soon I'll bring your supper."

"Yes, Angustias, yes."

"But first I want to introduce my little granddaughter," and she motioned to Cristina to come close.

Cristina walked as if before an altar. She was terrified of the old lady's hands, almost transparent on the edge of the sheet. And she felt even more terror when one of those hands raised up to find her and pat her.

"Her name is Cristina."

"A pretty girl."

When she felt the old lady's hand, it seemed to Cristina that a fish was grazing her cheek.

"Give Doña Luz a kiss, child."

Cristina leaned over the bed to kiss her forehead. She was revolted by the wrinkled skin, the watery, yellow eyes without eyelashes that seemed to look through things, and the vague smile.

"Did your daughter come, Doña Luz?" Angustias asked in a tone that suggested a trick.

"Yes, Luisita."

"Luisita, of course. Is she well?"

"Fine. With Tubby."

"Tubby. What a handsome boy. By now he's very big."

"Ve-very big." Her eyes were searching, as if she were talking with a shadow.

Cristina saw herself in the mirror on the wardrobe and again felt a slight dizziness. Was that herself? Standing there with her hands clasped over her stomach, near an ancient-looking bed where two old women were talking and remembering, their reflection seeming to fade away?

Yes, herself, there.

"Well, Doña Luz, I'm going to get your supper."

"Yes, Angustias, yes."

"A little *atole*?"

"Yes."

"I'm also going to put some alcohol on my scratch. Look."

"Ugh, ugly."

"I did it down below in your garden."

"Io-iodine."

"Yes, later. Right now I'll just put some alcohol on it. Cristina will stay with you."

Cristina's thumbs drummed rapidly on her stomach. She looked with pleading eyes at Angustias, who reinforced her order with only a nod of her head as she went out.

They were silent, although Doña Luz kept looking at her and smiling.

"In the wardrobe," Doña Luz said after a few moments.

Cristina remained quiet, turning up her hands in question.

"There," Doña Luz said with a movement of her chin toward the wardrobe.

"Should I open it?"

"Yes, yes." Her smile grew wider, and a small gleam crossed her eyes.

Cristina obeyed. She had the feeling she was opening a casket, and she looked at the row of old dresses as if they were ghosts.

"Up above."

Cristina looked at the shelf in the upper part of the wardrobe.

"In that box?"

"Yes, yes."

She had to stand on a chair. Lips trembling, Doña Luz watched her movements.

Cristina brought the box down. The dust made her cough. She opened it with the fear she'd had on entering the room, as if inside she might find something beyond imagining. Even though the old lady's smile and even her confusion were gaining ground, Cristina's confidence was growing. She put the lid on the floor carefully, as if it could disintegrate, and lifted the tissue paper. Inside were a straw hat with a veil, a notebook with blue covers, some peacock feathers, a photograph album, and a doll.

"How lovely!" she said, picking it up with both hands as if it were a baby. It had a muslin dress with lace on the sleeves and at the neck; rosy cheeks that contrasted with the pallor of the rest of the face; and curly, blonde hair.

"She's very beautiful." Cristina added.

"Beautiful, yes."

Turning, she saw Doña Luz was weeping. Cristina's smile evaporated and she put the doll on her shoulder, as if the movement might have hurt her and stimulated the old lady's crying.

"It's yo-yours." Doña Luz said from within her tears.

"Mine?" The smile reappeared, covering her face.

She hugged the doll firmly, and looked at her as if questioning her.

"Oh, how wonderful!" she added.

"The pictures."

"Would you like to see the pictures?"

Cristina felt obliged to do whatever she wished. She left the doll on a wicker rocking chair and went to get the album. Doña Luz took the album with a sigh, put it in her lap, and untied the blue ribbon. Emotion increased the trembling of her lips, pushing out her lower lip. Cristina felt her fright fading at last, giving way to a sad, salty tenderness that burned in her eyes like the dust from the wardrobe.

Doña Luz showed her the yellow snapshots, with edges eaten away by time, of a blonde woman with gentle eyes in full skirts and a man with hair slicked back, posed as if looking over his shoulder.

"Me. My husband."

"What a handsome couple!"

In one they were in the leafy garden paths near the stone fountain, which Cristina recognized and pointed out, saying, "It's down below!" to Doña Luz' smile of agreement and enthusiasm; in another they were seated on a small stone bench looking at the sky;

in another he was smoking a cigar behind a huge rolltop desk; in another she, with a listless air as if she were about to faint, by the trunk of a eucalyptus tree; in the breakfast room on the terrace, he with a forced smile, she pouring from an elaborate teapot; in the country, hand in hand, their heads leaning together and, behind, the wavy profile of some high mountains.

Doña Luz' eyes found the stability they had seemed to seek, and she pressed her lips together so her tears rolled slowly over her cheeks. Cristina looked at her, she herself almost crying, and went a little closer.

"Now, now, Doña Luz. Don't cry. I know how you feel."

But the picture at which both had paused thoughtfully was one in which the woman appeared much younger, in a batiste dress, and seated on the lap of a gray-haired gentleman with a stern look.

"My Papá," said Doña Luz, pointing to it with a wrinkled finger.

Cristina's heart skipped a beat. The young girl—how old was she, seventeen, eighteen?—had her arm around his back and her glowing face on her father's shoulder, as if holding him close, softening his apparent firmness, with a security of possession not reflected in the other pictures, and without that languid air that seemed to have overcome her.

"My Papá," Doña Luz repeated, outlining his profile with her finger.

Cristina put herself in the photograph, and it was she who was clinging to her father's shoulder, putting her face near his to gain from his strength, and with that peaceful expression that says all is well here beside you. She burst out crying openly, like Doña Luz, with a corollary cry, ageless, equally old.

16 **Doña Luz** closed the album suddenly, raising a light cloud of dust in which Cristina thought she saw memories and pain depart.

"I don't want . . . pictures," Doña Luz said. She sighed, picked up the ends of the blue ribbon, and began to tie them. "I'm crying."

"I cried, too." Cristina said and passed a hand in front of her eyes as if brushing away a spider web . . . She had not wanted to cry. One night she had sworn she would never cry again in her whole life. Papá had finished a long argument with Mamá by slamming the bathroom door, and Cristina felt a wave of anger rise to her lips, and she clenched her fists. Then she swore, no matter what happened, she would never cry again.

Doña Luz rested her limp hand on the album's leather cover and let her heavy eyelids close slowly.

"The . . . notebook . . ."

"You want me to get the notebook?"

"Yes," Doña Luz answered without opening her eyes.

Cristina went to get the notebook with the blue cover and took it to the bed.

"Would you like me to read it?"

"Yes."

"What is it?" She leafed through the pages: it was written in blue ink and small, tight handwriting with heavily marked commas and crosses on the T's, and some of the paragraphs underlined.

"Stories . . . She wrote them . . . Luisita."

"Luisita, your daughter?"

"Yes."

"Which would you like me to read?" Tiny stains had diluted the ink and turned it to a very pale blue.

"It doesn't . . . matter."

"They're very long, Doña Luz. We won't have time."

"Some of it."

"Well, but I can hardly make out the writing. Let's see the end of this one. Wherever . . . she went she asked for it. And nobody . . . knew what to tell her. What kind of tree? And she kept on asking . . . I can't understand it here, Doña Luz. It says something about . . . I don't know. Then she traveled . . ."

Cristina heard Angustias' voice calling from the first floor and it was as if her mind came back to reality. What was she doing there? She left the book open on the bed and stood up, tense.

"Señora is calling me. We have to go. It's late."

Doña Luz seemed not to understand and reached toward the place where the child had been, stroking the air. The shawl fell off her shoulders.

"Stay here . . ." Her sad, trembling smile was meant to be an invitation.

"I can't, Doña Luz. Really."

"The end . . . of the story."

Cristina looked toward the door with anxious eyes.

"Well, quickly."

She sat on the edge of the bed and fixed the shawl on Doña Luz' shoulders. Angustias was yelling at the top of her lungs downstairs, calling her. Cristina picked up the book and continued reading.

"Let's see, where did I stop? Now I've lost the place. Anyway, I'm just going to read the very end. By herself . . . she traveled through the world. I don't understand very well what it says here, either. Something about rivers. Many years passed . . . and she found it . . . in the deepest part of a forest . . . and she said to herself, I knew the tree of desire, of desires . . . that they told me about when I was a child . . . existed here. And . . . the child was no longer a child, but an old lady, tired of . . . I think it says searching, Doña Luz."

Angustias' shrieking could be heard closer. Perhaps she was coming up the stairs. Intermittently, Cristina looked toward the door.

"She had searched for so long that . . . I don't understand anything clearly here at all, Doña Luz. Then, among the other trees . . . she recognized it immediately, as if it had . . . always been near . . . And she was . . . very sorry . . . because the tree was as old as she was, about to die . . . as if it had been aging . . . at the same time . . . and she said . . ."

Angustias exploded into the room like a tornado, screaming and waving her arms around. Cristina and Doña Luz shrank back, looking at her, terrified. The notebook fell to the floor.

"You stupid brat! Do you think you can ignore me? Didn't you hear me calling you? Do you want them to find us here? Get downstairs right this minute!"

"Angustias," Doña Luz said.

"I'm going to take my doll."

"You're not going to take anything! And least of all that filthy doll that's so bulky." And she grabbed her by the arm before she could pick up the doll from the rocker.

50

"I want my doll!" Cristina cried in a voice that was almost a moan as she dodged away.

"See what I'm going to do with this worthless old thing," and Angustias tore off the head and threw it through the open window, letting the decapitated body fall on the floor. Cristina stared as if she could not believe it, and Doña Luz bent forward in the bed, trembling so hard her lower lip seemed to come loose.

Then Cristina screamed a muffled, "Nooo!" and attacked Angustias, her hands whirling like windmills. Angustias seized one arm, pulling her hair until the child began to cry.

"We're leaving here right now if you don't want me to pull out your hair!"

"Angustias," Doña Luz said, her eyes jumping from one object to another.

17 **Angustias stole** silver place settings, candlesticks, porcelain figures (which broke along the way), linen napkins, jewels (very few), a portable radio, a cut-glass centerpiece (which also broke along the way), a white silk dress, and a leather suitcase in which she put everything, which Cristina had to carry on their flight and even on the bus that took them back to the alley. Twice she dropped it—with a crash of breaking glass—and said she could not carry it anymore, her arm was asleep and her hand was cramping. But Angustias' blows on her head were so violent and her threats—opening and closing her fingers—so unbearable, she had to draw on strength from who knows where. During the ride, Cristina sighed deeply, thinking about the doll she had lost, which she immediately considered among the favorites of her whole life. She felt such hatred for Angustias that the idea crossed her mind to speak to her father to have Angustias put in jail—they might even torture her. But it was an absurd solution because Cristina would also be punished, and—even worse—she would have to go back home. It was better to wait, rescue Joaquín, take advantage of the first opportunity she had to escape and, before leaving, see what dreadful thing she could do to that horrible old hag.

Joaquín was not in Angustias' room, and while the woman was opening the suitcase and repeating her vulgarities upon discovering the broken porcelain and cut glass, Cristina ran to Jesús' room. Before she got to the door, she heard her brother's muffled cry like the final wail of a siren.

The boy was alone, tied by a rope around his waist to the latch of the bathroom door. He had bruises on his cheekbones and mouth, and he held up his arms when he saw his sister, with a cry that was like a delicate thread caught in his throat.

Cristina knelt down, hugged him, and cried too.

"I'm not going to leave you alone again, little brother. I swear I'm not going to leave you alone, even if they kill us." She held him close to her, ran her fingers through his hair, kissed his neck and the bruises on his face. Feeling safe again, the child regained strength and cried even louder.

She could not untie the rope, and Joaquín did not help her. He clung to her tightly, motionless. Then she heard the noise of bare feet on the floor and when she turned around, she saw against the light the man called Jesús, standing in the doorway, his hands on his hips—a foreboding image that no longer astonished her or brought on such fright that she could not even move, and from that moment on she was certain that anything could happen. Cristina guessed he was drunk again from his body's unsteadiness and his brutal look, which she could hardly see but could feel above her. Her anger for what he had done to Joaquín was transformed into sudden fear and the overwhelming need to get her brother out of there.

He took a few steps into the room. Cristina felt that, barefoot, his presence was even more violent.

He sat down heavily on the cot and searched for the pack of cigarettes in his shirt pocket. He lit a match and held it in front of his eyes, looking from behind it with a damp smile at Cristina, as if through a wall of fire. Then he lit the cigarette and took a long drag. He exhaled, watching the smoke blow out and disappear above.

"What did you say your name was?"

"Cristina." She stood like a wide-eyed doll.

"Ah, Cristina. Your brother is a nuisance. I had to go out for a while. But we played." And, turning to Joaquín, "We played, didn't we?"

"Stupid," said Joaquín without looking at him.

"He called me stupid. Did you hear him, little girl? He called me stupid."

There were sparks in his eyes. His cheeks, in contrast, seemed to dissolve, as if they were of wax and were near a fire.

"Why did you hit him?" Cristina asked, her voice softened by fear.

"For being a nuisance, what else?"

"He's very little."

"That's the reason I tied him up. I had to go out for a while."

"And you hit him."

"He didn't want to stay by himself. He's a stubborn child."

If Joaquín had been untied, at that moment Cristina would have grabbed his hand and run away with him.

"Help me untie him."

Jesús opened his mouth again in a broad smile, like a half-moon.

"Brat," he said showing her the end of the cigarette, "I didn't come to untie him. I came to tie you up. You hear me, brat? That's what Angustias told me—go tie up that brat while I buy a couple of things."

"I'm not going to escape. If my little brother is tied up, I couldn't escape."

Rounding his lips, he exclaimed, "Oooh," and leaned back against the damp wall. In addition to the cot, there was only a chair and a small table with a plastic cover and an almost empty bottle of tequila. In some spots the tiles had come up and you could see the loose earth. Above the bed, an ostentatious Christ figure with a heart in flames.

"You're a smart kid. That's for sure. You could untie him while I sleep, and escape. Right?"

"I can't untie him, really," she said holding her hands open. "I tried to, but I couldn't."

"Let's do something better. Come lie down with me here," and he smiled wider and patted the pillow. "OK?"

Cristina gulped as much air as she possibly could and held her arms out from her body as if she were about to fly. But she only let her arms fall to her waist and again breathed with difficulty.

"OK?" He looked as if he were spying through a keyhole.

"All right," Cristina said with a fleeting smile that took away the air she was breathing.

"Come here, then." He smoothed a place on the bedspread with an open hand. "Beside me."

"Sissy, I'm hungry," Joaquín said.

"My brother is hungry."

"Later! Come here now."

"Go to sleep for a little while, Joaquín."

"I don't want to sleep!"

"Go to sleep for a while!"

"No!"

"Joaquín . . ."

The child sat down on the floor, curled into a ball, with a look of resentment that made him seem even smaller. The rope wasn't long enough for him to lie down.

Poor Joaquín, Cristina thought.

"Come on now," the man said in a tone that was both demanding and suggestive.

Cristina went over hesitatingly, as if minimizing the importance of the event. She stood in front of him and watched him half-close his eyes and make his lips round, simulating a kiss. Repulsion was concentrated in the taste of her saliva. Then the man winked an eye and held out his hand.

"You right here on this side, little girl." The "little girl" increased her fear until it was unbearable, and she thought of running away, even though she would have had to leave Joaquín there. But she only retreated a few steps and buried her chin slowly in her chest.

"Come on, little girl. On this side."

Cristina lay down on the side by the wall, with the feeling that she would die if the man touched her. She kept her sight fixed on an undefined spot on the ceiling, her fingers clasped over her abdomen and her heels together. She was very pale, and her posture made her seem close to death. But when she felt the warmth of his wet kisses on her neck and his alcoholic breath, what happened in her body was a prolonged shudder that raised goose bumps on her skin.

Jesús' hand went down to the child's waist smoothly, his fingers playing as if on a keyboard, and stopped at her knee, communicating a blind, brutal desire.

"Little girl."

Cristina bit her lips until the pain overcame her fear and the heat of the man's hand on her skin.

"No," Cristina said.

She heard his weak laughter as his hand moved up to her thighs in a slow, wavy caress, as if on the surface of water, making her close her eyes, squeezing the lids closed. White lights like doves crisscrossed inside her.

"No," Cristina said. She expected an unbearable pain, but did not know why or when. Tears seemed to flow because she was closing her eyes so tightly.

Then he saw the tears and said, "Ahh." His mouth was close to her ear, and he only had to raise her face a little to wipe them off.

"Poor little girl."

The tip of his forefinger ran over her cheeks and lips as if outlining a new shape. Cristina opened her eyes and felt the fear leave her stomach when she heard Jesús weeping too, with a guttural cry that went deep inside and seemed to drown him. She saw his hand twitch in front of her and fall to his chest, losing strength in blows like the final beats of a large heart, until it fell still, the fingers spread wide.

"Oh, Lord, Lord, Lord," casting his eyes backward to see, foreshortened, the face of Christ above.

"Would you like for us to pray together?" Cristina asked in a low voice.

Jesús turned his back on her without answering. Then there was a silence that buzzed in Cristina's ears, and was broken when he began to snore.

18 **Angustias burst out laughing** like a gust of wind that blew the curtains and stirred up the dust in the corners. A fresh geranium was in her hair. She was carrying a bag with groceries, a bottle of rum, and, over her arm, the dress she had stolen from Doña Luz.

Hearing her, Cristina dreamed the devil was blowing on her with his offensive breath that burned like fire—tall, with skin of redness incarnate, standing in the doorway, just the way Jesús had been.

She awakened suddenly, sat up in the bed, and looked all around. The presence of Jesús at her side renewed the fear in her stomach, mixing with the discomfort of hunger. Joaquín was sleeping, seated on the floor, so peaceful, with his head resting on his crossed arms and his legs drawn up, like a small animal resigned to its fate, finding refuge in a deep, anonymous sleep.

"Get up, you lazy bums. We're going to have a party."

Angustias put the things on the table and gave Jesús a slap that startled him but did not quite awaken him. He changed position, and his snores became a weak gurgle.

"My brother is hungry."

"I brought ham and cheese and juice for my beautiful children." She threw a kiss with the tips of her fingers.

Changing position again, Jesús let his hand fall on Cristina's thigh. It revived in her the feeling of having him caress her. She looked at the hand carefully as if she could find in the rough knuckles, the dirty fingernails, the thick, black hair on the dark skin, an explanation for what she had felt. She threw her head back and frowned, sure that something was beginning to clear up. But after touching her, he wrinkled his nose and pulled back his hand as if getting rid of an attached animal. He drew in a deep breath that seemed to find obstacles on its way to his lungs.

"Aren't you ever going to wake up, Jesús?" Angustias asked as she took cans out of the bag.

Cristina looked at the man's face the way she had looked at his hand. The greasy lock of hair on his forehead, the line of drool running down from the corner of his mouth, the eyelids heavy with sleep. Why had that face suddenly become so important to her?

She got up and went to wake Joaquín.

"We're going to make some tortas like my children have never eaten before."

19 **Cristina and Joaquín** were seated on the floor, round-eyed, watching them and laughing nervously. Angustias' face was heavily made up and she was wearing the white silk dress, bursting at the seams under her arms. Thin, faded feathers were in her hair, and large gold earrings in her ears. She was making gestures as if she were a great lady in front of Jesús, who remained very serious with the long-handled mustache she had painted on him.

"Is the count here?" she was swinging her hips and fluttering her eyelids.

"I am the count," in a hoarse voice with arms crossed.

"Well then, look, I came here to screw . . ."

They both burst out laughing.

Joaquín felt as if he were in a theater, and he was taking small sips of pear juice. He laughed only when his sister laughed, but hearing a burst of laughter, could not help but imitate it.

"That's funny, Sissy."

On the table there were cans of juice, pieces of bread, half an avocado, and an empty bottle of rum.

Earlier, Angustias had taken off her clothes in front of them to put on the dress. When she uncovered her small, very white, flabby breasts, she winked at Jesús and took the nipples in the tips of her fingers. Cristina had never imagined that a nude woman could be so skinny and so ugly, with those sharp bones showing under the wrinkled skin. The man put on a black tie that he took out of a cardboard box with dirty clothes on top. He was taking long swigs of rum while Angustias was painting his mustache and the children were laughing.

Angustias and Jesús were dancing, throwing their feet up high and making obscene gestures between laughs and shouts, or caressing and embracing and then drawing apart to pretend elegant manners.

The radio was playing a romantic melody with soft, smooth modulations that contrasted with the brusque movements of the couple.

Suddenly Angustias turned and directed a brutal look, ringed with thick, dark circles, at Cristina. Was it the look of a clown or a witch? A witch disguised as a clown, Cristina thought, and was more afraid than ever.

"The little girl is going to dance, too, right, little girl?"

"I . . . I don't know how to dance."

"Dance with me. I'll show you how, little girl," and she held out her sharp hands, that under the light of the bulb seemed transparent, bloodless, purely bones.

Cristina found herself enveloped in a whirlwind of laughter and music, arms that seized her and lifted her up into the air. The looks of the man and the woman blurred together and awakened the same shudder she had felt when he caressed her. If she had been told such looks could wound your body, she would have believed it.

"And also you're going to have a drink with us," Jesús said when the music stopped, pointing at her with an enormous finger that seemed to push between her eyebrows.

"There's no more rum," Angustias said, pouting like a spoiled child. "I want some more rum."

"Ah, Jesús always . . . gives pleasure," and he raised his finger like a lightning rod. From under the cot he pulled out a bottle with a thick yellow liquid that reminded Cristina of a sick person's urine.

"What is that?". Angustias asked with a look of nausea.

"Different things. Rum and whisky, among others," he said, holding it up proudly, with a smile that showed his uneven teeth.

"Rum and whisky?" the woman asked with the same repugnance.

"And other things."

Cristina got the liquid down her throat with difficulty. It burned her and made her dizzy at the same time. Then she saw how Angustias and Jesús were drinking it in tiny sips, their faces distorted even more, until he threw the empty bottle against the wall and gave a shout of pain and glee at the same time.

To a new, strident melody they started dancing again, staggering around and bowing to each other with obscene gestures. They insisted that Cristina imitate them, learn the steps and whirl around with them. They put their hands under her dress, kissed her mouth and neck, and yelled in her ears. The girl felt like she was doing a somersault and could not tell whose fist hit her face and knocked her against the wall so she shrank down with closed eyes and hands clasped at the back of her neck. (Inside her there was a kaleidoscope growing in brilliance.) When she opened her eyes, Jesús and Angustias were embracing. He was laughing:

"Are you mad? Are you really mad, Angus . . . ?"

She tried to scratch him, but he held her hands and kissed her mouth. Her makeup was running. She yelled as he was kissing her. When they separated, she spit on him. A thread of blood ran from the corners of her mouth. Then she lifted his shirt, pulling it out of his pants. With her fingernails she dug into a piece of the dark skin on his shoulders and he let out a long moan that made Cristina think of a wolf's howl. Now it was Angustias who laughed, showing her teeth. Cristina went over to her brother and hugged him. Joaquín was trembling and watching the scene with eyes that made Cristina remember another scene, joining it with the present. Papá and Mamá were fighting during supper—Papá hit the table hard, turning over the pitcher of milk, and Mamá started crying—and Cristina went over to her brother's chair and embraced him as she was doing now, protecting herself in protecting him, confident that as long as they stayed that way, no harm could touch them, and it would finally go away. Jesús showed his gums, threw back his shoulders, and tilted his hips toward Angustias with a back-and-forth movement as if he were going to dance again, while she continued spitting on him and digging her nails into him even harder. Cristina saw the movements of their waists and wondered if they were going to make love again, in front of her and Joaquín. She remembered something soft and sweet that she had seen when they made love the night before, in contrast to the fear awakened in her now, as if they were not the same people, or the same act, or something was added.

When Jesús hit Angustias the first time, the girl closed her eyes, and when she opened them, the woman was on the floor, moaning quietly. He kicked her face and stomach while asking her:

"You . . . ?"

The blows on Angustias' bones made a noise like the sound of glass breaking. One kick after another, with the speed of an old movie. She shrank so much with each spasm of pain that it seemed she was going to disappear. Without missing a beat as if delivering another blow, he reached toward the table and picked up the knife Angustias had used to cut the bread. He knelt down and, directly under the flood of very bright light, raised the knife. Cristina screamed.

20   "Hug me tight, Joaquín."

Cristina had the feeling she was going to faint. She seemed to be going down a narrow tunnel, with the hum of a freezing wind hurting her ears.

"Look, Sissy," Joaquín said.

He pointed to Angustias, whose whole body was shaking as she tried with both hands to pull out the knife stuck in her chest. The man was gone.

Cristina stood up and went toward the woman, holding onto the back of the chair.

"Help me!" Angustias said in a very thin voice, her teeth chattering. Her mouth was twisted up, and thick drops of sweat were running down her forehead. Because of her excessive makeup, it looked like she was acting.

Cristina knelt down beside her, took the handle of the knife in both hands, and pulled it out, causing a profuse hemorrhage. The bloodstain extended to her shoulder and neck, sticking her dress to her body.

"The louse . . . is going to pay . . . for this," and she tried to kiss the cross, but her hand did not reach her lips, falling motionless on the wound in her chest.

Then Cristina felt a curiosity that overcame fear. She gazed into the woman's eyes as if into a well and saw how death was coming near and gradually overtaking her. The brightness was fading, and she seemed to see things the girl could not see. It was so strange—

almost entertaining—like when she saw her make love with the man who had now killed her.

"Son of . . ." but a final rasping breath brought death suddenly, settling into her eyes, which were fixed on an indefinite spot in the ceiling. Her chin jutted toward her contorted forehead and left her mouth open, as if the word she was about to say kept her from closing it.

21 **She cut the rope** with the knife, staining her hands with blood. Joaquín kept on crying and moving around, and she begged him:

"Joaquín, help me. That man is coming back . . ."

The boy insisted:

"Wanna go ho-o-ome!"

Outside it was a windy night without moon or stars. The sheets hung on the lines seemed to be ghosts heading for them, swaying. Cristina walked firmly, dragging Joaquín along into the cold.

"We have to go in for the sweaters," she said, looking fearfully at the door to Angustias' room. She turned the handle carefully. The cats meowed, and Cristina felt their scratches on her legs. She picked up a box of matches from the table and lit the candle. The cats' eyes glowed. They're furious, she thought, and embraced Joaquín to protect him.

While getting the sweaters off the bed, she saw the folded newspaper with her picture. She took it close to the candle. Joaquín's picture was also there, and it said, "Disappeared yesterday . . ." So that meant . . . Cristina shivered.

"We have to hurry, Joaquín."

Before leaving she looked around the room. Her eyes fell briefly on the oval picture of Angustias' mother on the dresser, enveloped by the gloom in a thick, reddish aura. She sensed a certain resemblance between the two women, and a bitter flavor rose to her mouth. Poor thing, she thought.

It was drizzling. Cristina felt the drops of water like tiny needles on her cheeks. She buttoned Joaquín's sweater and put on her own.

Turning the corner, they saw Jesús, very close to a streetlight, his open shirt coming out of his trousers, a lock of wet hair on his forehead, and the high points of his mustache beginning to dissolve. The rain—shining in the neon light—made him look as if he were on the other side of a fine mesh curtain. He gave the impression that he did not dare cross the street, and merely thrust his head forward and then turned around, swinging on his bare feet like those dolls on a round base that never quite finish falling. When the children began to run in the opposite direction, he saw them and yelled,

"Hey, you little brats . . . !"

Cristina knew he was not going to follow them, but they ran for three blocks, very close to the wall. The few people they met looked at them for a moment and then continued on their way. When Joaquín couldn't take any more, gasping for breath, they had to stop. They sat on the steps of a building and breathed in the icy air.

"I don't want to run anymore!" Joaquín said.

Cristina was also out of breath, even more than when she was running. She could not get enough air, and looked upward to draw in more. Suddenly she did not know what to do. She hit one fist against the other and cried with anger, catching her tears with the back of her hand. Impotence only increased her feeling of rebellion.

"I'm cold, Sissy," Joaquín said shivering.

22 **They walked** to a boulevard—Joaquín dragging his feet and falling asleep, his teeth chattering because of the cold. Cristina hailed a taxi and asked the driver to take them to the train station. The cab driver looked at them astonished in the rear view mirror.

"Where?"

"To the train station," Cristina insisted, while she tried to dry Joaquín's head with the edge of her skirt.

"What are you going there for?" the driver asked as he started the car.

"My parents told me . . . They're waiting for us. They talked to me and told me . . ."

"Alone? At this hour?"

"That's the way my father is," Cristina said.

The driver raised his eyebrows and accelerated.

"Do you have the fare?"

Cristina took a hundred-peso bill out of her purse and showed it to him.

"Look."

The car moved on down the avenue, and Cristina sighed. Joaquín was asleep on her lap. He was soaked. Cristina stroked his hair, hoping her caresses would also help to dry him.

"Are you going on a trip?" asked the driver, and his eyes in the rearview mirror had a penetrating look that Cristina shrank from. She said only, with emphasis:

"That's the way my father is."

"I know. But I'm asking you if you're going on a trip."

"Yes."

"Is he your little brother?"

"Yes."

"Being so wet will make him sick."

"No."

"The things you see . . ." and he began to explain how he cared for his children.

Cristina was looking at the palm trees in the median, frosted by the rain. She thought it was as if a hundred years had passed since she left home.

When they got to the station, Cristina awakened Joaquín and gave the hundred-peso bill to the driver. He gave her the change and insisted on going with them, but Cristina said no, no, thank you, got out of the car, and ran with Joaquín, asleep on his feet.

23 **Cristina entered** the noisy station looking down at the floor, certain that everyone had seen her picture in the paper and would recognize her immediately. The promise of chocolate candy had enlivened Joaquín, and now he wanted to climb onto a porter's dolly. She took off her sweater, and then took off her brother's; both were soaking wet. They went up the ramp and into the waiting room. Joaquín began asking where that man was going, and that one.

"Joaquín, don't point at people!"

"Where's Papá?"

"Papá isn't coming."

"I want him to come . . ."

"You and I are going to get on the train by ourselves."

"But I want Papá to come. And Mamá."

"They're not going to come."

"But I want them to."

"You have to understand that they are not going to come. And you're never going to see them again. You're going to live with me. You and I, by ourselves. We're going far away on the train, as far away as we can."

"I want my Mamá!"

"Well, you're not going to see her. You only have me. Do you understand? We're all alone. We don't have anyone else. You only have me, and I only have you. We're going to travel together and grow up together. I love you more than anyone in the world, and we're never going to be separated."

"And Papá?"

"Papá is dead."

"He's not dead!"

"Yes, and Mamá, too. They died, and we don't have any parents."

She bought two chocolate candies and put them in her purse to keep "for later," when they got on the train, in spite of Joaquín's protests and foot-stomping.

"Look, Joaquín, you're going to obey me. *I* say when we're going to eat the candy."

"I'm hungry."

"Me, too. But first we have to get on the train."

There they were, behind the glass on the platforms, sparkling under a blue light, with long lines of happy people getting on them. Their windows were like invitations to a lifelong dream. Opening the paths to the ends of the earth.

The problem, clearly, was the ticket. But if she could manage to get on one of the trains, Cristina was sure she could find somewhere to hide and a way to fool the security guards.

Getting onto the platform was simple. "We got off to buy some chocolates," she said, and showed them.

"And your parents?" the official asked.

"There," Cristina said pointing to the trains.

And they passed through.

She felt an intense desire to run to the nearest train and get on it. They could hide in a bathroom or in the dining car, or simply walk down the aisles until they would be far enough away from the city. However, it was better to know where a train was going and when it was leaving. And above all, to get on just when it was about to leave; any earlier would be taking an unnecessary risk.

She chose one that was going to Chihuahua and would leave in half an hour.

She went up to the front of it, looking at it knowingly, as if just getting off rather than about to get on. She imagined herself already in the dining car, having breakfast with Joaquín the next day. And the money to pay for it? And how to explain when asked about their parents? But that was not important now. Anyway, she would see. As she would have to see what kind of work she could get in Chihuahua, and where she could leave Joaquín meanwhile. Surely she could find someone to trust . . . Passing by a small window in which some silhouettes were outlined, she imagined how it would be to sleep there, hugging Joaquín close, frightened by their aloneness but happy, raising the shade in the morning to see the landscape, the cities they were passing.

She looked up and saw beyond the roof of the platform, a piece of the sky, impenetrable, intact.

That was when she heard Joaquín's cry: "Papi, Papi!"

24 **Her heart stopped** when she realized what was happening, and then beat rapidly, more rapidly than ever, when she dared to turn around and look where her brother's finger was pointing. She gulped a mouthful of air and let it out with a sharp wail as she dropped the sweaters. Papá was running toward them, smiling and calling them by name. Joaquín went to meet him with open arms:

"Papi, Papi!"

Cristina raised her hands up to her cheeks as if she were going to scratch them and looked all around everywhere, sure there was still an exit. She ran toward the end of the platform, shoving people and sobbing with, at times, a muffled Noooo! Papá was coming ever closer, calling her:

"Cristy, my darling little girl!"

A woman tried to stop her, but Cristina gave her a kick and ran faster. Every time she turned around, she was sure that Papá was no longer there, no, the nightmare would end by going away, that nightmare like a bird of doom that had always followed her, and was now taking the most horrible of its forms, the only unbearable one. Because in spite of the fact that she had managed to jump from the platform to the gravel and was running down one of the tracks, stumbling on the railroad ties, skinning her knees, but getting up immediately to continue into the darkest part of the night, Papá had finally reached her, and her kicks and cries of no, I don't want to, I don't want to, no, would be useless because Papá knew how to control her, to carry her, to press her against him, hold her legs with one hand, and make her lose strength little by little while saying:

"My darling, Cristy, it's all over, all over."

SERAFÍN

Deserted streets, monocular lighting.
                                    At a corner,

the specter of a dog.
        He searches, in the refuse, for

a phantasmal bone.

—*Octavio Paz*

For Matilde Aidée

1 **Serafín watched sadness** move into his house the night Papá left. Papá had been drinking all afternoon, as usual in those days, and as soon as night fell, he got up with difficulty, took his poncho from the spike that served as clothes rack, and said, I'm going to Mexico City to see if things go better for me there because here they are as bad as they can get. In the heavy silence his kiss on Mamá's forehead sounded more like a complaint than a caress. Serafín and his brothers were watching, sitting on some torn, lumpy straw mattresses. A hazy light from a kerosene lamp hanging from the ceiling swung back and forth, creating long shadows like tall phantoms on the adobe walls.

After he left, the only sound was Mamá's crying, deep, slow, guttural. Bent over the table, her distorted face in her hands, her eyes that seemed to follow Papá wherever it was he had gone.

"Your papá has gone away, Serafín," she said in a voice like a thread interlaced in her crying.

"Yes, he's gone."

"And there's nothing to do."

"Yes, Mamá. There's nothing to do."

With that nothing to do, she reacted. She passed her hand in front of her eyes as if removing a shadow and went with her children to pray below the picture of Jesus with His Heart in Flames that she had inherited from his grandmother, who had died in that same house of an illness called fright.

Serafín had felt more loving warmth from his grandmother than he had ever felt from his mother or father. But his grandmother had died of fright and now his father had gone away. The wind outside brought noise from a long way off, and he felt sadness expanding.

◆ ◆ ◆ ◆

In Aguichapan the people were best at growing corn, but that year the crop had been very poor. They ate what they could and struggled along. Serafín's papá had walked all over the area looking for work until he was worn out. He sold chickens and straw hats in the market, worked as a peon building a dam and drilling a tunnel. He even went as far as Tierra Blanca to cut cane. From one place to another, following the hopes and rumors of work.

"They say there's something over there, I'd better go, even if it's far away."

Or:

"Right here in the next town, some streets are being paved."

Serafín went with him because he had stopped going to school ever since his father had a fistfight with the teacher in the cantina after a bitter discussion about politics, one of those in which no one agreed.

He had hardly begun to make out the meaning of letters, but he liked the mystery that surrounded them. It was much more entertaining and less tiring than working in the soil. Who would enjoy and not get tired of carrying a basket full of sombreros on your back for hours and hours? Or walking and walking along the grassy foothills on the way to possible jobs, better than the ones before but almost always nonexistent, the mirages of bad times. And returning by the same empty road, with more dust in your eyes than going, just the two of them, father and son, their only company the occasional passage of a drove of pack animals, as forsaken in the world as they were.

Papá would say:

"I'm not going to let myself rot here in Aguichapan. Better to die right now."

So he looked for work outside. His hope was always outside of Aguichapan, away from the people of Aguichapan. A dumb bunch, he used to tell them.

◆　◆　◆　◆

One starry night when they were crossing a river on a barge, sitting on the boxes they had to carry to the other shore, Papá said:

"I have to go to Mexico City to see what's there."

It was the first time Serafín heard that such an idea had occurred to his papá.

"Lots of people go and never come back," Serafín told him, taking refuge against his father's strong chest, trying to get inside.

"And the reason is there's work to spare there."

Serafín tried to imagine Mexico City while he breathed in the air of the stars falling over him. And a strange sensation, close to happiness, invaded him, as when he spent too much time looking at the star-filled sky. The barge proceeded slowly across the dense water.

When he was tired, his father felt the need to drink. Even the little money Uncle Flaviano lent them went entirely to drink. He collapsed on the table of unpolished pine that stuck splinters in your clothes when you brushed against it, looking at things only he could see.

◆　◆　◆　◆

Days later—without Papá the days got mixed up, sadness made them all seem the same—Mamá explained to him and his brothers that it was not true that Papá had left with another woman, as they were saying in town. He went in order to better himself. There in the city there was lots of work, and soon he was going to come back with a lot of money and presents.

"He's thinking about us," Mamá said in a voice not even she believed. "Even though he's far away, he's thinking about us."

Serafín felt a red flush rising to his cheeks and, although he did not want to say so, said:

"He took Cipriano's daughter with him. On his way to the highway, he went by for her and took her with him. Leo told me."

"It's gossip," she replied, putting a sharp note in her voice.

He just put his face down to hide.

Not until he was alone could he cry while looking at a sad afternoon.

In the distance the horizon was no more than a smooth line of copper wire.

◆　◆　◆　◆

The strong winds went away, it rained, and there was a calming, iridescent light, with the earth smoothed out, covering itself with dry leaves. But contrary to what Mamá thought, Papá did not come back. Things were getting worse for them. And nobody would lend them anything. It was the same for all the people in Aguichapan, because they all asked each other but no one had anything to lend.

So he decided to go to the city to find his father. He was the oldest son, so he was the one to do it.

At first Mamá did not want him to go.

"I've already lost your father. Now I'm going to lose you."

Then she agreed, as if by then everything seemed to be the same to her. Or maybe because she knew where her husband was living in the city and she hoped if his oldest son arrived looking for him, he would change his mind.

"Here, look for him with this man, at this telephone."

She prepared a bag for him with a little food and a letter in an envelope.

"Give this to your papá yourself."

It was some time later before Serafín knew what the letter said, but he held it up before his eyes so much he almost guessed what was in it.

2 **One morning at dawn** Mamá crossed the thick layer of frost, stepping firmly on the polished flagstones, holding Serafín by the hand. The burro drivers were lining up their animals in pairs to transport water, and the crestfallen branches shed drops of dew. The crowing of the cocks scared away the darkness. In some windows Mamá felt the presence of eyes spying on her. In others she saw them clearly, looking out through a crack in the curtains, ashamed, luminous in the ashy light that was dawning. Damned people, she thought, and continued thinking damned people until they reached the highway and stopped near a tall pine that seemed to pierce some transparent clouds galloping very low. Serafín clutched the plastic bag to his chest, his sleepy eyes red, making him see things in a thick, unreal haze. He saw how the sun came up suddenly between two hills, already in its fullness, with the rapid flight of the immense darkness.

Two buses passed without stopping. Serafín told his mother none was going to stop, but now she was the one who had decided her son should go. Her expression hardened and she assured him one would stop, there was always one that stopped.

"They've already seen us come here to wait for the bus. Now you have to go."

"What are you going to tell them?"

"Nothing. I'm not going to tell them anything. I didn't tell them anything when your papá left, and I am going to tell them even less now that you're going."

"They're going to ask you."

"But I'm not going to say anything. And I'm going to stay so far away from them, they won't be able to ask me, and if they ask me, they are going to get tired of asking."

"And Uncle Flaviano?"

"The same thing. Nothing."

"You're going to need him to lend you some more money."

"We'll see."

"You're not going to talk with anyone, Mamá?"

"With your brothers and sisters. Why talk with anyone else until you and Papá get back?"

"We're going to come back, Mamá," he emphasized it to get rid of his doubts.

"Of course."

She was quiet for several minutes, as if she were somewhere else, already settled into the silence she would be living in for the coming days. As if past, present, and future had already started getting confused.

The sun was rising, brilliant, completely round, hastening the morning.

"There comes another bus," she said taking a few steps toward the highway, ready to stop it however she could. And she stopped it. Maybe it was going to stop anyway, but just in case she went out onto the highway and waved a white handkerchief high, like a dove.

75

She cried, telling her son good-bye. But she cried more inside than she showed. She embraced him, hugging him more closely than she had for many years, while the driver yelled as hard as he could,

"Come on, come on! Hurry, Señora, or I'll leave . . ."

Really, she shed hardly any tears. She was going to say something, but just pressed her lips tight and put them on her son's cheek in something meant to be a kiss. Her lips were cold, and Serafín felt that the coldness in his mother's lips was the real good-bye. Why at that moment did he remember the little girl who had died in the river years before? The driver revved his engine without moving and said, "I mean it, Señora, I'm leaving." Mamá said a blessing behind Serafín, but could not make the sign of the cross on him because he went up the first step with his back to her, went off thinking about the little girl who had died in the river.

"God bless you, Serafín!"

◆   ◆   ◆   ◆

He got on the bus and looked at the aisle dividing the seats as if it were an aisle in a dream. From the back pocket of his pants he took out a bill and, staggering, gave it to the driver. Then he stumbled over the packages on the floor, crossed the hurdle of sharp looks and took a seat in one of the back rows. They had left him a seat with a window, and when he looked back through it, he saw only a piece of land and underbrush left far behind. He thought his mother would already be far away and felt the urge to get up and yell to them to let him get off, where was he going without her, but settled for hugging the plastic bag against his chest and clenching his teeth. Now there's nothing else to do, he told himself.

But he could not stop thinking about the girl in the river. Why did she die? She just slipped on a rock and fell on her back, hitting her head. Can people die because of something like that? Only a moment before they were sitting on the bank. She was barefooted with her legs stretched out, her feet very white, like two little shining fish. Serafín's mamá and the girl's mamá were in the water with their chemises white and floating out like balloons.

"Come on," the girl's mamá said with a sparkle from the sun in her smile.

"The water's fine," Serafín's mamá said.

"Timid kids."

The sand was shifting under Serafín's feet. He saw when the girl climbed on a big, fat rock and when she tried to jump to another, like the first one and only a step away. She held out her little hands as if she were going to take flight and then fell on her back with the water caressing her, peaceful, indifferent. They carried her out, her eyes fixed on an indefinite point in the sky, her very white legs dangling like threads.

For a long time Serafín looked at her in the coffin within the circle of candlelight, surrounded by the hushed murmur of prayers.

"Look at her for the last time, my son, because you'll never see her again," Serafín's mamá told him, wrapping the "never" in a sob as she held a handkerchief to her mouth.

She was wearing a white dress and had her hands crossed over a crucifix on her chest. Serafín tried to imagine what her closed eyes were seeing and felt it was something sweet and far away. He could almost see it himself, but what was it? He looked for it in her eyelids, in the soft lines of her lips, in those hands like wax. What was it like to see death?

In the moment before he left the coffin, something like an answer came to him, a slight ringing in his ears, an unknown flavor in his mouth, a figure that was forming in the swaying smoke from the candles and coming up from the box. He was certain she would continue to be the same, wherever she was, and that her face would always keep that tranquil serenity of lilies.

3 **The passenger next to him** was an old man with shriveled cheeks and a humpback, who was doubled over himself. Was he sleeping? Even though Serafín noticed his eyes were open, he wondered if he was asleep because nothing else in his face showed any sign of life. What did he look like? A scarecrow. But Serafín was looking at him with such questioning eyes, the old man turned and smiled, which made him seem even more like a scarecrow.

"Hello," he said.

"Hello," Serafín answered.

Without shifting position, tossing his words toward the open area formed by his thin, half-open legs and occasionally looking at him sideways, the old man added,

"Are you going to the city?"

"Yes."

"What for?"

"To look for my papá."

"Do you have any relatives there?"

"No."

"Where are you going to live?"

"I don't know. First I'm going to look for my papá."

"And in the meantime?"

"Well, I'll see. Wherever I find myself."

"You won't find anyone there."

"I have to go."

"Do you have any money?"

"Not very much. Some that was left after paying for the bus." Serafín patted his pocket to be sure it had not fallen out when he got on the bus.

"You're dead."

"But I have to go, Señor. Really."

"OK, go, then . . . go to hell!"

And he said no more. As if he had gone to sleep with his eyes open. Serafín felt a strange shiver, more in his bones than in his spirit or on his skin, and did not know if it was because of the old man's curse or because the farther the bus went, the farther his mother was left behind. He leaned up against the window and pressed the plastic bag against his chest, as if in doing so, he could grasp a little of what he was losing. He looked through the window to have something to do, but without paying attention to anything, overcome by what was happening inside him, with a great desire to cry but confident that if he did, everyone in the bus would turn to look at him, pointing at him, perhaps laughing at him. So when the countryside became cloudy and he caught a salty tear in the corner of his mouth, he lowered his head like the old man beside him and raised the bag until it covered his face. What would they look like, the two of them bent over the same way? What would all those people in front of them think?

That was what always happened to him. Mamá would scold him and he would listen to her scolding with tight lips and then go somewhere to cry for a while. Only a little while, and he went back ready to put up with more scolding. Something happened with tears, although they were very embarrassing, especially in front of strangers. But all curled up like that, at least they would not see him. The memory of that cold kiss he'd received from Mamá overcame him suddenly and brought on a long sob. He imagined her staying behind, standing on the highway at the same place where they'd been waiting for the bus, her figure becoming smaller and smaller until it was a meaningless point, lost in the shimmer of the coming day. He did not see Mamá, he could not see her once he stepped onto the bus, but he was sure she had waited a long time. And he imagined how she would have seen him just as he would have seen her, the images blending together, both going unavoidably farther from each other, each one becoming smaller and smaller for the other one.

◆ ◆ ◆ ◆

He closed his eyes, and sleep began to drag on him. A dream that came from the night before and did not let him awaken completely in the morning. He had gone to bed early, but as he dozed off, he saw Papá come back. He heard it distinctly when he opened the door, and then saw him, taller than usual, enormous, in the opening of the doorway. As tall and dark as the shadow made by the swaying of the lamp. Smiling, with the night coming in behind him, letting in a cold wind that made Serafín shiver, though it did not interfere with his joy in seeing Papá finally return, so he pushed back the covers and sat up on the mattress.

"Papá!"

And it was then he realized it was not true. He'd dreamed it, or better said, he'd almost dreamed it because he had not yet slept.

The door was closed, no one had entered. A bit of empty night filtered through the window, without Papá.

"Go to sleep now. You have to get up early in the morning," Mamá said, sitting at the table as if watching over Serafín's sleep the last night she would be by his side.

"I saw Papá come in very clearly, Mamá. Very clearly."

"I also see him every once in a while, but it's pure imagination. If he'd really come in, we'd know for sure he'd come."

"I was sure he came in."

"But there's no one. Look."

"Yes."

"Go to sleep now."

"And you, Mamá?"

"I'm going to sleep in a little while. I was just waiting until I got sleepy."

He was not going to ask, but bit his lip and dared.

"Were you looking toward the door when I saw Papá come in?"

"I looked at you, and saw you see something I didn't see."

"So nothing really happened?"

"Nothing."

"It was only a dream?"

"You had hardly started to sleep. Those dreams are the trickiest. Now go to sleep."

Obediently, he closed his eyes, and a multitude of images came to him. A young Mamá laughing with Papá. Mamá putting a flower in her hair in front of the mirror. A young Papá kissing her on her neck. Papá drinking and talking to Mamá in a voice rising in tone until it hardened into a smothered yell. Mamá listening to him in silence from the corner, where there is a hearth of bleached clay, stirring the pot of coffee, blowing on the coals to revive the embers, or going to tuck in one of Serafín's brothers, the smallest one, who is wriggling like a little snake on a mattress close by. And Mamá saying, I'm dead tired, going to the bed—a metal one, the only one in the room—and undressing in front of them, while Papá takes a drink of tequila, his eyes gleaming. He stands up, caresses her, and whispers something in her ear, laughing nervously. But Mamá rejects him, and Papá returns to the table to talk to himself. He talks and talks in a monotonous voice that ends up lulling Serafín. At times, when he is angry with Mamá, he yells and hits the table with his fist, threatening to destroy everything, everything, and Serafín never understood very well what that everything included. But sometimes those quarrels finished with Papá waking him up and asking him to keep him company because he felt so lonely. Serafín would sit drowsily at the table, pulling the quilt around himself and holding his face, his sleepiness, in the palm of his hand, and Papá would tell him, as before, about the trips he had made and how Mamá did not love him, kept him suffering here, and he would put his hand between his legs as if to comfort himself.

4   **A hard jolt of the bus** woke him up. He looked all around and rubbed his eyes. The old man was sleeping beside him with his head thrown back. Serafín thought if he were dead, he would not look very different. His sharp chin stuck out in front and from his thin lips came a snore that was a muffled whistle.

How long had he slept? The sun already seemed high and there were no clouds in the sky. Occasionally the dense, deep green hills revealed the wavy line of the horizon.

By now he must be far away, and going farther all the time. Where would it all end? Who would be there? In the town's plaza, for instance, that now would be beyond all those hills, lighted by a different sun. He had crossed it so many times, without thinking about being there. Just crossing it. The shadow of the jacaranda trees was falling on the benches of polished wood, and the old people were sitting in its shelter to watch the fountain with three jets and the people passing by. Those old folks. He saw them . . . Would they be there now?

What did he dream? He only remembered a street, or something that was more like a tunnel of oaks or poplars making lines in the sunlight. And someone was running there. Yes, it was himself. His figure came clearer as he remembered the dream. He was in the city, on a street in the city—that was the feeling—and he was running to meet someone. He was going to find him but he bumped into another man. A man who stopped him and held him up in the air. An old man, skinny and tall . . . He pressed tightly against the window when he realized he had dreamed about the old man in the next seat, and about the city. Why, since he had just met him? Why had he gotten into his dream? He blinked and felt again the same shiver he had felt when he got on the bus. It seemed that the worst thing was to sleep, as always. Why was sleeping always the worst thing?

◆　◆　◆　◆

"And if I do it, Mamá? Ask them to let me off and take a bus going back? It's going to be easier now than later. And Papá has to come back someday, doesn't he? And if not, at least I would be with you. Why should I leave you to go look for him? I wouldn't be alone. I would be with you, even though not with him. What I would like is for the three of us to be together. The way it is now, I don't have either of you. I'm not with you or with him. And I'm not going to have either of you when I get there—that place they call the city."

◆　◆　◆　◆

The only specific information he had about the city was from a certain Felipe Hurtado. He remembered him very well because he and Papá got drunk together one night and that was all they talked about.

"It's hell there, Román. I swear it's hell itself. You've only gone for a visit and then come back. But stay a little while to look for work and you'll see. For weeks I walked around like a fool, knocking on every door I could find, asking for work or at least that they would offer me a lousy tortilla—that's how broke I was. A tortilla, damn it, I'd take anything, and nobody gave me a thing, Román."

"Hell doesn't exist," Papá answered, missing the whole point, simply because he could not bear a religious reference.

"As far as I'm concerned, God can . . ." he said one night when Mamá and the children were praying in front of the image of Jesus with His Heart in Flames, and although he did not dare say the whole sentence, he made an obscene gesture. Mamá only lowered her head and pressed her lips together, as if the prayer might have

choked her. She took Serafín's hand, because he was the child clos-
est to her when they were praying, and said, let's continue, full of
Grace, the Lord is with You . . .

"Didn't you hear me? I said, as far as I'm concerned, God
can . . ."

But Mamá interrupted him, turning around and looking at him
with eyes burning as if just lifted from the embers, leaving him pet-
rified in the middle of the room.

"Be quiet! Or go away so we can finish praying!"

Papá was very drunk, and when he quieted down, even his eyes
cleared up, as if Mamá's words—like part of a prayer—had awakened a sudden feeling for the sacred. But the reaction was worse.
He burst out laughing and went to urinate in the doorway, there
in front of his wife and children, who continued praying. He leaned
his body back as if bending over double and threw a spray upward,
straight up, while continuing to laugh. Serafín could not forget how
he laughed while urinating and Mamá kept on praying, Blessed art
Thou among women, and Blessed is the fruit of Thy womb, Jesus.

"Go to Mexico City and you'll see that hell exists, no shit," Felipe
Hurtado replied, taking a drink of his warm beer.

"Well, look, Felipe, as far as I'm concerned . . ." Papá answered,
beginning to drag his words, as if they had to run an obstacle course
before they got to his lips.

"You're talking just to talk, Román."

There was a long silence in which they just drank, leaning over
the pine table.

"I think . . . sometimes I think hell would be better than here,"
Papá said a moment before his head fell from his hand, rolled down
the length of his arm, and hit his forehead on the table, with a noise
that made Serafín think of a rock falling from a high place and split-
ting in two. Papá's head split in two, Papá without a head, Papá
divided, never again the same old Papá. That night Serafín waited,
watching for Papá to stand up and go to bed, with his head whole,
as if nothing had happened. Before Felipe Hurtado left, he took
his jacket off the spike—a jacket of green corduroy that he had
brought from the city and that he showed off every Sunday strut-
ting around the plaza—as he muttered,

"You're screwed, Román."

And he left after five warm beers and several more tequilas. Serafín counted them, one by one. He also counted the last one, which he drank while Papá was asleep on the table. And he heard him sing:

"Open the door, my darling,
open, open, open,
I brought you a little something,
nice, nice, nice."

5   **Serafín looked** at the dust on his shoes that, he thought, was already dust from far away. He took a piece of bread with cheese and beans out of his bag and ate it quickly so he would not awaken the old man and have to offer him some. Hateful old man. Then he felt around in the bag until he found a can of juice and drank it, staring blankly through the window. The trees were going by unchanging as if really they were only one, repeated over and over until he was tired of it. Things farther away looked normal by moving more slowly: the adobe houses in the tiny villages, the grazing animals, the human figures with hardly time to strike a pose, like in the game of statues. They passed by, chasing each other without ever catching up.

He finished eating and put the bag near his feet—touching it with his calf—and instantly fell into the deep sleep of an ancient fatigue.

◆ ◆ ◆ ◆

Now it was the cold light of the moon that filtered through his dream and finally awakened him. He opened his eyes and saw it, very low, with its halo of thin clouds. Startled, he sat up and checked on the presence of the bag. At his side, the old man was sitting up very straight, looking wide awake, his profile showing clearly in the gloom, like the edge of a hatchet.

"What happened?"

"What do you mean?"

"Are we there?"

"No. We're stopped."

Serafín looked out the window and saw a mass of shadows in the distance, lights blinking off and on in the underbrush, like watching eyes, and the nocturnal movement of the trees. There were small groups of people by the side of the road.

"A wreck," the old man added without changing his position, without even bothering to look at him. "The bus hit a car. It seems some people are hurt. Everybody got out to look, but it doesn't interest me. All accidents are the same."

"And . . . very long ago?"

"We've been stopped here for hours."

"And what about me, Señor?"

"What about you?"

"Was I asleep all the time?"

"You didn't move. I even got close to make sure you were breathing. You never know with the heart."

"Could you die that way, asleep?" Serafín asked in a tone that combined fear of death with fear of the old man himself.

"You can die any way. I had a friend who died while he was eating, with his spoon in front of his face and his arm up. And I saw a child jump from a chair and when he got to the floor, he was dead."

"Why?" he asked, pressing up against the window with his head down in his collar, hiding his fear.

"I told you, the heart stops whenever it wants to, right then, because of bad air or bad thoughts. There are thoughts that can stop the heart instantly."

"And dreams?"

"Dreams are very dangerous for the heart. I've learned to wake up from dreams that would have killed me like lightning."

Serafín remembered that, when asleep, the old man had really seemed awake, or rather, half dead.

"Is all that true?"

"I never tell lies, child," he answered, now looking straight at him, with eyes that held the gleam of forged steel and made Serafín huddle even closer against the window.

"Don't talk to me about that anymore."

"What do you want me to talk to you about?" he asked, stretching out his bony, clawlike hand. Serafín finally hid himself in his collar like a turtle, and the old man gave him a light knock on the head. "'Oh, don't talk to me about that, Señor.' Aren't you a man?"

"Talk to me about something else, Señor. Please."

"What, does death frighten you?" the man asked coming close with his dark smile and sour breath, like a whiff of hell itself.

"Can you tell me about the accident?"

"I didn't see it because I was asleep, too. But the screams woke me up. There was a lot of confusion. A woman got off to walk around and was almost run over by another bus. Just because she wanted to get close and see. A fat man pulled out a badge and yelled that no one should move until the highway patrol came. The children were leaning halfway out the window. The bus driver was afraid and took off running, but the fat guy with the badge caught him and brought him back, twisting his arm."

"And now?"

"I think we have to wait for an ambulance. Get out if you want to. You're a child."

Serafín put on the sweater he was carrying in the bag. He was about to leave his seat when the old man asked with teasing eyes if he should take care of the bag. Serafín rejected the offer with an emphatic "no" and a shake of his head. So the old man, smiling broadly and showing two decayed teeth, reached out his big, bony hand to take the bag. Serafín jerked the bag away with a brusque movement that made it hit the metal edge of the window and produced a noise like broken glass.

"It was a joke, boy, go on."

Before getting off, Serafín sat in one of the seats in front—almost all were empty—and took out what he was carrying in the bag: the shirt, the clean underwear, the folded pants, the paper sack with the food, some cans of fruit juice, his cup and ball game, and the wooden car. He reached all the way to the bottom and found the tiny plaster virgin that his mother always had near her bed. It was broken in two.

Why did you put that there, Mamá? And what should I do with it now? He held the two parts together and looked at it sadly.

It's the thing that belongs to you most, isn't it, Mamá? One day you said that you always had it with you. That ever since you'd prayed with your grandmother, you prayed to that virgin. You put it in the bag so you would almost come with me yourself. Why, if you knew it would break and I can't even pray by myself? Remember I can't get the prayers out.

6   **He got off** and went to stand at the edge of the highway. Fog dissolved the outlines of everything. People were coming and going, talking quietly, complaining in their looks and gestures, going back to the wrecked car to see what they had already seen, moving around and blowing on their hands, drinking coffee from a thermos bottle. The wind produced the sound of waving stubble.

Serafín went toward the car. There were two people stretched out beside it, a woman covered up to her neck with a coat and a man who was holding up the nails of one hand as if to scratch the air, moving his head from side to side, licking his lips and moaning:

"Enough, for God's sake, enough . . ."

The woman was curled up like a sleeping child. Her hair was a wet, red stain that ran down one cheek to her neck. Her eyes half-open, her lips purple, thick. In the air Serafín heard the same buzzing as when the girl was in the river. Or was it only fear?

A few minutes later, the ambulance arrived with its siren screaming and a red light that tore open the cloak of cold. Serafín moved away and went toward the bus, where he saw the old man get off; the shadows and his loose clothing made him look even more like a scarecrow. He walked with long strides and his head swayed as if it were hung on a wire. He threw a cigarette butt in the air, turning it into a shooting star, and went deep into the underbrush, toward the moon, until the night swallowed him up. Serafín followed him, the dry leaves crunching under his light steps. Where was the old scarecrow going? Impossible not to go find out.

Coming from behind a tree, Serafín saw him from the back standing in the round frame of the moon, his figure lengthened by its light.

"Come here," he said without turning around.

Serafín took two steps backward. His eyes were like tropical fire beetles.

"Come on. I'm urinating and you'd better do the same, you impudent little snoop."

❖ ❖ ❖ ❖

Their arrival in the city kept him from staying quiet in his seat. The moon dissolved with an iridescent tranquillity as soon as the first houses appeared. The lights followed each other like a procession of torches, more and more intense. Now he was there, with no way to avoid it. This was the city. He almost stood up in his seat, but the old man pushed him back down.

"You're disturbing me, you stupid brat! You're like a grasshopper."

The bag fell to the floor with a dry thud, and he imagined Mamá's virgin broken into countless pieces.

"It's the city, Señor," Serafín said in a calmer voice to make up for his excitement.

"I already know that. But wait to get off."

Serafín continued watching through the window with the same astonishment, his nose plastered against the glass, smearing it, his eyes huge to take in everything.

The lights finally hypnotized him, making him feel elevated above what he was seeing. He could not move. He knew he should not, because the heavy hand of the old man would subdue him immediately, but in spite of that, or perhaps because of it, something inside him came out as a sigh.

There were the lights below, and not above, him.

As far as he could see, there was the city, as he had so often dreamed it. He saw streets, houses, many things. He flew over buildings, came down in a wide street, and walked in it as if on water, with wings on his feet.

❖ ❖ ❖ ❖

When they got off the bus, the old man told Serafín to follow him. Being in the whirlpool of people was very different from the earlier sensation of being up above. He was lost in a forest of legs, guided only by the old man's high, hunched back.

"Señor, Señor!" the hunched back was hidden behind a column and suddenly, no matter how hard he hurried, he could not see it.

"Come on, hurry, run!"

He began looking in the dizzying gallery of faces for Papá's, as if he were here, about to start back to Aguichapan just as Serafín arrived. Among those crossing like shadows; among those dozing in their seats, their sleep protected by the uproar; among those lining up to buy a ticket; among those on the platform, just about to get on a bus. And if he should find him? How would it seem? And how would Papá react upon seeing him?

"Where are we going?" he dared to ask when they were on a wide street like a raging river.

"To my house."

They got on a bus that stopped on every corner and had standing room only. Serafín wanted to talk to his father on the phone just as soon as possible. Why had he not done it in the station? Why did he always forget the most important thing? But he had felt so bewildered that he was only now beginning to react. The old man was holding him up by the neck, choking him.

They got off when they got to a park. It was a park with loose dirt and taco stands all around, enveloped in clouds of smoke. The neon lights silvered the dry branches of the trees making them look like phantom watchmen.

"Señor, I need to make a phone call," Serafín said, pulling on the old man's jacket.

"There are no phones around here."

"But I need to do it. I came to find my Papá."

"It's almost midnight. You can talk to him tomorrow."

"But I want to."

The old man held his arms up high, waving them around like a large bird.

"Go on then!"

Serafín lowered his head and looked up through his eyelashes.

"I . . . you'll have to dial the numbers for me. I don't know how to read them."

"I'm not going to dial anything. Understand? It's very late and you're going to wake people up. Tomorrow is as good as today."

"What if my Papá leaves early in the morning?"

"Where does he live?"

"I don't know."

"What do you mean you don't know? Where are you going to call him?"

"At a number my Mamá gave me."

"Show it to me."

Serafín felt in the pocket of his shirt. He pulled out a wrinkled, yellowed piece of paper and showed it without letting go.

"It's just a name and number," the old man said, bending over it.

"I have to find him here."

The old man burst out laughing and threw up his arms again, stirring up the air in the park.

"Stupid brat. And what if he doesn't live there anymore? What if he went to live somewhere else? How are you going to go back? Tell me, how?"

"I don't know . . ."

"Look, tomorrow is another day," and he put his hand in Serafín's hair and ruffled it up, as if he meant it to be a caress. "We can get up early and call him from a store that's next door to my house. OK?"

"All right."

"That's more like it. Now we can go to sleep. That bus was hard on my bones."

7 **They entered a narrow, dark alleyway** with water-stained walls and overflowing garbage cans. They crossed a patio with washtubs and clothes hung to dry. The doors were metal, and the few lighted windows gave a murky light. At the end of the patio, the old man stopped and took out a key chain.

"You can sleep here tonight and do whatever you want tomorrow."

"Thank you, Señor."

The old man lighted a candle. Its light barely edged around

things, which seemed to float in the darkness—the table, the chairs, a rusty metal bed with a wool spread so tattered it seemed about to come apart, a worm-eaten dresser with a small lace cover on it, and the oval picture of a smiling old lady. In a corner, near the bathroom door, cans and empty bottles and a pile of yellowed newspapers.

"Your house is nice, Señor."

"It isn't my house. Well, it is now, but before it belonged to a woman called Angustias, who died. These are her things. The lady in the photo was her mamá."

Serafín went over to see the photograph, which seemed to glow.

"She looks like my grandmother."

"Sit down," the old man said, pointing to one of the chairs and going to the dresser to get a bottle of rum. Then he took off his jacket, his sweat-soaked shirt revealing his long backbone, like a skinny cat. At the table he lit a cigarette and smoked it, taking in long drags and letting out dense columns of smoke that seized and finally overcame the light of the candle.

"There's nothing to eat. I don't eat much."

"I brought a little something. Want some?"

"What do you have?"

"Cheese and bean tortas and canned fruit juice."

"Then give me a torta."

Serafín put the plastic bag on the table and looked for the tortas. It was difficult because all his moving around had made them fall out of the paper bag. He found them on the bottom, after taking out his clean underwear and his ball and cup game.

"What do you have there?"

"Just a few things. And keepsakes."

"And what is that?"

"A virgin my Mamá put in for me, but it broke. I'll see if I can glue it together later on . . . although it's broken into a lot of pieces."

And as he looked at the detached head of the virgin, his eyes seemed to be praying to it, as if he suddenly remembered all the times he had seen his mother praying to it.

"There's no point in praying to a broken virgin. I suppose, I don't know."

"My Mamá loved her a lot."

"Then keep the head at least. It will help you remember when it was whole."

Serafín gave the old man a torta, and he took one also. They ate without saying anything in the smoke and the viscous light. The old man took a long drink straight from the bottle, and small flames grew in his pupils, as if the light that surrounded them had been put into his eyes.

"What happened to that woman you said was the owner of this place?"

"They killed her. Right here."

Serafín's mouthful caught in his throat. The old man noticed it and put his hand on Serafín's, imparting a sticky, repellent warmth.

"Do you want me to tell you about it?"

"No, not really."

"They stuck a knife in her."

"They did?" Serafín said, keeping his eyes in the shadows.

The old man came close, with a smile darkened by the candlelight.

"Someone who loved her a lot, who would have given his life for her . . ."

Serafín yanked his hand away suddenly and stood up.

"May I use your bathroom, Señor?"

There was no answer. Serafín took the candle and left the old man in darkness, with his eyes gleaming and the cigarette burning on the edge of the table. In the bathroom there was a dirty basin, a medicine cabinet with a broken mirror and a toilet without a seat. Serafín looked in the mirror, and took a moment to recognize himself. Who had told him that if he looked at himself that way by the light of a candle for a long time, he would end up seeing another face, all of the faces there had been in his previous lives? How many faces had he had? How many Serafíns had there been before this Serafín? And who had told him that? Surely his grandmother, who was always interested in such things. And she'd died from one of them. She had this peculiarity of talking to herself, wherever she was, and once when she had come back from bathing in the river, she said:

"I don't have anyone to talk to anymore. My soul has gone into the river because I've looked at myself in it so much."

From then on she was sad. She hardly ate anything and seemed not even to breathe. She stayed in a chair, lost in her shawl, just a shape, not seeing or saying anything. She, who had been such a talker.

The doctor saw her and diagnosed the same thing they saw: melancholia. He asked her some questions, made some jokes with her, and she insisted that her soul had gone in the river because she had looked at herself in it so much, and she no longer had anyone inside to talk to. He prescribed some pills but it was impossible to get her to take them. Mamá treated her like a child, talked to her full of smiles, and put a pill on her closed lips. Even with all the stories she told her, and even at times hard-eyed threats, the pill did not go in or if it did, it came back instantly, covered with saliva, but completely whole. The same thing happened with food. Sometimes, very rarely, a bit of chicken broth or atole went in, as she kept poking the spoon at her.

So Mamá went with Serafín to see the priest. Half-opened shutters let almost no light into the sacristy. The short, gray-haired priest, who was almost deaf (ideal to hear confession, they said, if you just mumbled the sins very, very softly), received them smiling and invited them to sit down on chairs that were high and had feet like claws. Even the penetrating odor of the place seemed strange to Serafín. What could the shining chasuble laid out on the chest of drawers have to do with him? Or the photograph of the Pope, touched up to the point of caricature? Or the large cup and the sprinkler, like decorations on a corner table. Serafín had never gone to Mass. Papá had forbidden it. He could pray at home as much as he wanted with his Mamá and brothers and sisters, but not set foot in a church. Never in the church. In a tone that left no room for doubt, Papá said the church poisoned the soul.

Mamá almost shouted telling the priest about Grandmother:

"She just sits in a chair all day without saying or hearing anything. I don't believe she thinks anything, either, because you can't see any thoughts in her face."

"She might be possessed," the priest answered, with one hand up to his ear to catch the words.

"How can we cure her, father?" she asked, taking a handkerchief out of the pocket of her dress because she already felt on the verge of crying.

"By praying for her, and talking to her a lot about God. There's no other way. If you like, I can come talk with her."

"Father, I'm having problems like you couldn't imagine with my husband. I think he . . . is the one possessed by the devil . . . I'll wait for some day when he's far away to come get you and take you to see my poor mamá."

Then Mamá took Serafín through the chancel to the altar, as she was saying, look, my son, look, it's the house of God, because she was overcome with crying and had to turn away.

"Come on, you keep vigil. I'm too sad. I'll wait for you outside. And cross yourself."

Serafín stopped in front of the altar rail. He crossed himself and looked at the tabernacle; the large crucifix, chipped and leaning over so far, it seemed about to fall; the window panes with scenes of the passion; a ray of light that filtered through a very high niche to put the final touch on a wall covered with images of dull gold . . . Was it really the house of God? Mamá assured him that it was. And if it really was? He began a prayer, but could not remember how to continue. That first visit to the house of God was overwhelming, with so many things to learn. And going out, he went by the fourteen Stations of the Cross. He crossed himself and looked for the last time toward the altar. And he wondered, really . . . really, are you here?

8 **One morning** the priest stealthily entered Serafín's house—Papá was going to be away for two days—and sat down close to Grandmother to talk to her. But she answered in a voice so low, with hardly more than the movement of her lips, that the priest kept asking, "What?" So Mamá began to translate, screaming the nearly inaudible words Grandmother was saying. Even so, there was very little they could understand clearly.

"The river was flowing so slowly, I could see my face in it, just like in a mirror. I could see all my faces there. And the water carried them along in its slow current. It carried all of them along, even the last one, which was probably the face of my future life. Then, seeing it going away in the water . . . I realized my soul was there going away, too. I committed a great sin, seeing something I should not have seen. Because I lived in a short time what I had already lived for many years. Also I lived what I was going to live afterward. That's why my soul left my body, frightened by the sin . . ."

"But where did your soul go, Mamacita?"

"Yes," the priest said helpfully, "ask her where it went."

Grandmother sighed deeply, and her eyes sighed, too.

"Probably not even she knows."

"That's right, Padre, not even she knows."

The priest asked them to leave him alone with Grandmother. Serafín took advantage of the chance to play marbles with Leo. Mamá stood in the doorway with her hands pressed tightly against her mouth, her whole body rigid, as if she could hear what the priest was saying and it hurt her.

But Grandmother did not get any better. Worse than that, she was wasting away. The doctor came back and advised them to take her for an outing once in a while so she could get some fresh air. Uncle Flaviano got a cart and on Sunday mornings he settled her in it, all bent over, just a pile of bones, and took her for a ride in the hills. Serafín went with them once and realized Grandmother saw nothing in spite of all the things passing in front of her. She even ignored the aroma of the jasmines. And if she tried to respond to some kisses on her cheek from Flaviano's youngest child, her fleeting attempt at a smile turned into a grimace.

"Aren't we bothering her with so much carrying on? Maybe it's better to leave her in peace; she has her reasons for being the way she is," Flaviano said, and he stopped coming for her on Sundays.

However, he brought a *brujo*, who also made her go out, but only once, to the most likely place where she had lost her soul.

◆ ◆ ◆ ◆

It was late afternoon when Serafín saw the procession leave (even Papá and Flaviano's wife went). Grandmother was in her chair, enthroned on high, with the sun's final rays on her trembling white head. More than anything, it seemed like a religious procession, with her as the adored image. The *brujo* was carrying an incense burner, tortillas, eggs, tobacco leaves, and a bottle of tequila.

Mamá told Serafín later: the problem was to find the place where Grandmother leaned over to see her faces in the water. They took her to a place on the bank of the river, speckled by light and shadows. They kept questioning her, stopping from time to time; the *brujo* would check her pulse and stare into her eyes as if he were looking into a well. Finally, some time later, when the night was already well advanced, Grandmother's lips trembled and her hand came up to point to a large rock. Papá—who was carrying his own bottle of tequila—couldn't help applauding and crying out, "Hurrah!" Immediately, the *brujo* checked her pulse and confirmed that, indeed, that must be the place. They ate some of the food, and the *brujo* buried the remains near the rock, making a small mound. On top of it he put crosses made of the tobacco leaves and then drank some of the tequila and sprinkled some over the mound. Finally he talked to the moon, ordering it to return the lost soul to them.

All that must have done some good, because when the *brujo* opened his arms to the moon and was talking to it, tears came to Grandmother's eyes, and she kept on blinking. But also she went limp, turned a pale, greenish color, and her pulse beat wildly. They had to carry her home as quickly as possible, tied to the chair, her head swinging around so much it seemed to be coming off. They put her feet in hot water and forced her to drink some very strong tea.

The *brujo* came back by himself the next day at dusk with a stewed chicken. Fearfully, Serafín and Leo spied on him from a distant tree. Stealthily they watched him make signs toward the sky in the dim purple light, tear the chicken into pieces, eat part of it and bury the rest. He spent a long time kneeling in front of the small mound, waving his arms around wildly and saying some words they could not hear. Only when he passed close by them, on his return, throwing his fists from the ground up to the air, could they hear him exclaim:

"Soul . . . I bid you to come back. Come back to the body you left behind. Your body is waiting for you. Earth, leave that soul in peace, now we've given you food and drink. Moon, help us."

Who was it the *brujo* was trying to call up? Serafín tried to find inside himself that thing they called the soul. What part was it? Memories? Fear? Dreams? Maybe, since Grandmother had lost her soul, she no longer had dreams. Or was it like the pain of being stuck by a thorn?

One of those Sundays when they took Grandmother out in the cart to get some air, Serafín stuck himself with a thorn while cutting a flower. Grandmother was watching him, he was sure she was watching him, even if her eyes were vacant. A drop of blood came out of the tip of his thumb.

"Look, Grandmother, I pricked myself."

But she did not answer him. Even the drop of blood, and the ache inside from it, meant nothing to her. She, who had always been so concerned about anything that happened to Serafín or anything that might happen to him. Did losing your soul mean you also lost the ache?

◆ ◆ ◆ ◆

And one day Grandmother died. When Serafín got home, he saw her on the bed, the thin skin that was still on her bones looking transparent, her eyes closed and her mouth half-open, as if the last breath was still there inside. Mamá, inconsolable, knelt beside her, pressing her hand as if she would not let her go.

"She went with a smile," she told Papá, who, overcome with so much grief, had drunk too much and was swaying as he stood at the foot of the bed, with an expression as if he were denying death. "I saw her go with a smile . . ."

Later on, Serafín dreamt that Grandmother was still there and woke up crying.

"She's not here. She went to heaven with God the Father," Mamá had to say in his ear, rubbing his back, stroking his hair, and covering him carefully. "Your Grandmother died. She went to heaven and she sees us from there and helps us. But she's not here."

"And her soul?"

"It went back to her body. That's why she died happy."

"Did you see when her soul went back?"

"No, because you don't see the soul, but I saw her smile when she felt her soul enter her body again."

"What did she feel?"

"I don't know. Maybe something like happiness. And warmth. You saw how she was always cold lately."

But afterward, Serafín saw his grandmother not only in dreams but in reality. Until one night Mamá got tired of his visions and shook him firmly, taking him by the shoulders. They were near the door of the bathroom, where he said he had seen her. Papá and his brothers and sisters were sleeping. Mamá got up because she heard him talking in the dark.

"I was talking with her," Serafín said.

"You can't talk with her because she's already dead. You have to understand that."

"I heard her voice so clearly. Just as clearly as I'm hearing yours, Mamá."

That was when Mamá took him by the shoulders and shook him hard, as if to drive out whatever vision he had inside him.

"She's gone! Leave her in peace so she can rest!"

 When he came out of the bathroom, the old man was already in bed with the covers up to his neck and with a strange look, like a wrinkled child.

"Put out the candle and come here."

Serafín blew out the candle but stayed by the table. He again felt fear in his bones. In the silvery light coming through the curtainless window he could see the old man's frozen smile, very wide. Why was he more frightening when he smiled?

"It's better if I sleep in the chair. I can sleep wherever I am."

"Come to bed. It's very late."

He sat on the edge of the bed to remove his shoes and put the bag next to them.

"Take off your pants."

"This is how I sleep."

He lay down on the bed on top of the cover, as far away from the old man as he could. Who would have thought, with the repugnance he'd felt from the beginning, that he would end up sleeping beside him.

"You're a fraidy-cat. You're even scared of words."

"I've been thinking . . . if it's true . . . about the woman who died here . . ."

"Yes, it's true. I don't tell lies."

"And . . . you killed her?"

"Yes, but I'll tell you about it tomorrow. Go to sleep now."

The old man put his bony hand on Serafín's chest like a shackle and a few seconds later was asleep, snoring with that snore that at times turned into a muffled whistle.

Serafín looked at a piece of very blue sky through the window. Was it the same sky Mamá would be looking at? And what was he doing there, within the painful embrace of that crazy old man, without any certainty he would ever find Papá?

◆　◆　◆　◆

"Remember that night when I couldn't sleep? You were awake, too, and stayed with me the whole time. Then later, you were sleepy, but I couldn't sleep, so you didn't go away. You kept on hugging me and telling me things. How could you stand it, all night, your head nodding, leaning up against the wall, because, you said, if you got under the covers, you'd go to sleep? And why was I so bad letting you do that, making up visions so you would see how frightened I was? What are you looking at now, Mamá?"

◆　◆　◆　◆

He jerked awake some hours later, sitting up suddenly in bed. Where was he? He looked beside him at the old man, gulping in air that turned into snorts. He had dreamed something about him. Or was it about the woman who died there? The images were mixed together. Instead of a woman, the old man was killing a pig in the middle of the room, cutting its throat. And it wasn't here, in this room, but rather at his own house, outside his house. Perhaps because one time he really did see his Papá kill a pig. Seeing the blood spurt out made him feel sick. And even more when some skinny, stray dogs came nosing around to drink the blood that had not yet seeped into the earth. Afterward, inside the house the lard was boiling in a pot giving off a dirty, thick smoke. Serafín almost vomited when Mamá made him eat meat of the animal he had seen die. It's different eating an animal you know, one you've grown fond of just by seeing it.

He sat on the edge of the bed to put on his shoes. Picking up the plastic bag, he walked on tiptoe toward the door. It squeaked when he opened it, and the old man stirred in the bed. Serafín was going to leave when he heard the cracked voice, not yet awake.

"Are you leaving already, brat?"

"Yes, Señor."

"Go on, then."

The windows in the alleyway were dark. The sheets hung out to dry, moving lightly in the breeze, seemed to be about to take flight. He went out to the street, feeling calmer. Anything was better than staying there.

He walked to a park where the earth was dry. What time was it? A car passed by only rarely, making the street seem real. I'm in the city, he thought. The darkness and silence made him doubt it. He sat on a bench in the park and watched the night. There was no one there, nor did it seem possible at that moment that anyone had ever been there, except the wind. A wind that swept up dust, dry leaves, and pieces of newspaper, like a hangover from the day before. He felt as if he were alone, completely alone in the city.

He was hungry and looked in the bag for one of the cans of juice. There were only two left, but why think of that now? Hope was ebbing and flowing inside him, like an interior sea. And now he was feeling better, maybe because at last he was free of the old man. Also, he did not come to the city every day. He sighed and lay down on the bench. And, at last, he rested in a deep sleep with no visions, all by himself.

10 **At dawn someone woke him up,** shaking his shoulder. It was a policeman, who asked him what he was doing there. He sat up quickly and picked up his bag with both hands. He blinked, unable to concentrate on the question. Behind the policeman he saw the patrol car, with its insistent red light driving away the sun, just appearing.

"Yes," he said. "Yes, Señor."

"Yes, Señor, what? I'm asking you what you're doing here." His eyes were peering through narrow cracks, and he had a fuzzy mustache.

"I went to sleep."

"But why here? You should go home, go on."

"I'm from Aguichapan, Señor. I came to find my papá. I need to call him at this number," and he looked for the piece of paper. "Please help me . . ."

The policeman took the paper and smiled so broadly his eyes disappeared.

"Hey, Rigo," he said, turning toward the policeman who was still sitting in the police car, with the door open and his cap pushed back, his face indefinite in the hazy dawn. "He came to find his papá and needs to call him on the phone."

"At this hour? It's very early. Let him be."

The policeman twisted his mouth and returned the paper. Just as he saw him turn his back and head for the police car, Serafín heard him say something about filthy Indians who come to the city just to dirty it up.

Serafín was going to ask him again to dial the number, but his legs did not respond and neither did his determination, so he stood there, holding out the paper, watching the patrol car turn into a dark street as if into the last remnant of night.

◆ ◆ ◆ ◆

He spent the morning asking people to dial the telephone number. He kept on stubbornly, stopping people by tugging on their clothing, then shrinking smaller, looking through his eyelashes, and soft-

101

ening his voice to show his paper and ask his favor. Some brushed him off angrily, others did not even answer him, and others smiled and even gave him some money.

Only two women were kind enough to find a phone and dial the number, but there was no answer, and later there was a busy signal.

The wave of people and cars was growing as the day went on. At moments it stopped, as if drowsing, only to surge again, with more force. At first the uproar frightened him, but later, watching it entertained him. The eyes, the gestures, the cars, the buildings dizzyingly high, the shop windows, the newsstands, the children passing by him (what were their lives like?), the hard attitude of the people waiting for a bus, gathered for an indecisive attack on the still moving step, already past them as the anguished squeal of the tires grew louder. The stream of traffic, the horns, the wave of people going down into the Metro (where he, of course, did not dare go), the sun at its highest point, the panes of glass one after another like fugitive mirrors.

◆　◆　◆　◆

"That was the city, Mamá. The place my uncle Flaviano once said we didn't have any right to because we were just going to be a nuisance. Remember? You know he never wanted to come. He would rather die without knowing the city than be a nuisance. He was always like that, very dignified. Who would think that Ramona, his oldest daughter, the most spoiled of his twelve children, would die in the city of a very strange death. You didn't talk about it in front of me or else talked in very low voices, but I knew it was very uncommon because Aunt María said, what a peculiar death, poor girl, to end up that way. And I saw my uncle Flaviano cry in a different way. He cried and cried and refused to come to the city to claim the body. Why should I, if she's already dead, he would say. Better to keep her alive in me. So he never knew the city, since that was his best chance. It didn't tempt him, or he was tempted, but held out against it. You know how he is, Mamá."

◆　◆　◆　◆

He stopped in front of all the shop windows. It was where he lost most of his time. It seemed to him the show windows were more city-like than anything else. On an avenue with palm trees, there was a row of windows with everything imaginable, and some things he had never imagined. He went past them very slowly, taking in every detail. He looked through the windows just as he had looked through the bus window before arriving at the station. With the same eyes and the same astonishment, and it almost seemed to be the same window.

He gave a bill to a beggar woman with a child inside her *rebozo,* one of the last he had left. It was because of the way she looked at him. She said:

"Give me something from that bag you're carrying."

But he preferred giving her the bill. Then he thought it would have been better to give her a can of juice or one of the *tortas,* but it was too late. There was no way he could ask her for the bill and give her something else in exchange. Anyway, when he turned, she was no longer there, as if she had guessed his change of mind.

When it was afternoon, he came to a narrow, very green street with two lines of foliage joining in the distance. He sat down on the sidewalk and realized how tired he was. The sky's shimmering, cloudy surface was beginning to give way to night. He needed to insist on the phone call, but first he had to rest a little. And eat something. Why had he given her that bill? And where had that woman come from? Maybe from somewhere close to Aguichapan, and she was also looking for a relative. And it was then that hunger hit him.

And what if the same thing happened to him? How would he feel? He took the last *torta* out of the bag and ate it slowly, looking at a large tree that reached out over a high wall to keep him company.

11 **A young woman** dialed the number again, but it was still busy.

"Here, you listen," and she handed the phone to him. He had never talked on the phone, but supposed the repeated sound meant what they were telling him.

"Could you please dial it again for me?" he insisted in a voice that was no longer soft, but breaking.

"It'll be the same. You have to wait a while, see?" and she returned the paper to him.

He went to a park to spend the night. Now he was really sad, much more so than the night before. Although the night before it was as much astonishment or fear as it was sadness. In the park he recognized the old sadness at his side, the same sadness he'd seen grow in Aguichapan.

He remembered that Mamá had told him to change his shirt after two days, and it calmed him to obey her. It was better to do it there in the park and at night, although the cold made him shiver. He had put it on when he felt the cross in the pocket on the left side, the one closer to the heart. It was a small, metal cross with a Christ figure roughly embossed. Was it the one Mamá would put in Papá's knapsack when he went away, without his realizing it, until one day he threw it on the floor and threatened to break it? Although at that moment he thought it was probably one that belonged to his grandmother. Had Mamá put it in because he loved his grandmother? But what if he broke that, too, or lost it? Why had Mamá put in the cross and the virgin? He had a fleeting desire to react like Papá, to throw them away, since they only made him sad. Why would he want to have them with him there, lost in the city?

◆ ◆ ◆ ◆

"Cipriano's daughter. I told you what they told me, Mamá. And what if he really brought her to the city and is living with her? He might even want to go back with her, if he wants to go back. Think about what I'm going to ask you, Mamá: What if Cipriano's daughter came to live with us?"

◆ ◆ ◆ ◆

In Aguichapan, that was what happened to a friend of his, Alino, who lived with his father's two wives. Alino's father worked in buying and selling huge bottles of different colors, called *damajuanas*. But the way things had been going lately, he could not sell any. They saw him coming and going on foot to the villages nearby because his *burro* died and he could not buy another. He had a long pole across his shoulders with the *damajuanas* tied on, hanging like spheres. One day in May, a new woman arrived in Aguichapan from who knows where, and he moved her into his house as if it were a normal thing, just because he felt like it. Alino told Serafín:

"At first, my mamá put up with it, but now she says she can't stand it any more."

Serafín asked:

"Why does your Papá want two wives in his house?"

Alino just raised his shoulders until they almost touched his ears. That was in July. By September, a rumor was going around that Alino's mamá had murdered the other woman while her husband was on a trip, because neither woman was ever seen outside the house, and one night somebody saw a terrible, fearful silhouette outlined on the tattered curtains, with a knife held up high. That was how the rumor was born, and since neither woman left the house, they believed it. It grew, passing from mouth to mouth, but Alino's papá came back and to show it was not true took both women by the arm and walked them around the plaza on Sunday, even buying them ice cream.

One day Alino told Serafín:

"My mamá is going to leave home. She says now she can't stand my papá's other wife one more day."

"What does your papá do with two wives?" Serafín insisted.

"Things," Alino answered, as he shot a marble with his thumbnail.

On Christmas morning Alino's household awoke to a white cross painted on the door. There was a huge commotion that day because Alino's papá insulted everyone in the village right in the middle of church, making obscene gestures toward the altar. They started beating him up and Serafín's papá ran to help him because, he said, he also hated crosses and above all if a coward painted one on someone's door. Outside the church they got into a fistfight and shouted the worst insults, Alino's father and Serafín's against all the other men in the village. (Between his deafness and concentration on the Mass, the priest hardly noticed.) When Serafín's papá returned home, with his nose the color of a beet, he said that Alino's family, including the new woman, were going to move to another village close by, because they could not stand the people of Aguichapan anymore.

"That's what your filthy crosses did!" Papá yelled in Mamá's face. She just set her teeth as tightly as possible and continued fanning the coals again with a fan made of *petate*.

Now he had one of those crosses that Papá hated, crucifying the palm of his hand—maybe the very one Mamá used to hide in Papá's knapsack, with a Christ figure so poorly made, it did not seem human, just a rough shape. And he did not know what to do with it, because if he put it in his shirt or in the bag, he was sure to lose it. And what if he threw it away right now, here, into some underbrush?

12   **"You couldn't do it,** could you, Mamá? And anyway Cipriano's daughter is very young and very pretty and maybe she would be the one who couldn't live with us. What would she think of you? And what would you think of her? And what would the two of you think of me? Or my papá? What am I going to do if he's really living with her? Why didn't you ever talk to me about that?"

◆   ◆   ◆

Serafín still had the traces of lost sleep in his eyes as he looked beseechingly at the very tall, skinny man who was standing on the corner, absent-mindedly smoking.

"Señor, could you dial this number, please?"

The man almost doubled over to gaze into the misery in his eyes.

"I'll give you the money, look."

He took a coin out of his pants pocket and, with a quick, magician's movement, put it in the man's hand.

"But the money isn't the problem. Here, keep it."

"I don't want it. If you don't dial the number, I don't need it." It was a trick that had not worked, because they usually let the coin fall to the ground and at times even added a couple of pesos. "Everybody says they're in a hurry. But I'm also in a hurry—to talk."

"The problem is the telephone."

"There's one right there."

"Then, let's try." But that one was not working, and they had to find another one. They talked about Aguichapan, the trip, the accident on the highway.

The man dialed the number and asked for Serafín's papá. Serafín stood on tiptoe and stretched his neck, almost climbing up the man's back.

"He doesn't work here anymore. This past week he went back to his village with some relatives, but we don't know the names of the village or his relatives," a voice like sandpaper said.

The man told Serafín what was said, but Serafín became so distressed, the man dialed the number again. While he was doing it, he asked him:

"Who is the person you're asking for?"

"A friend of my Papá's, who lives here. My Mamá told me he'd offered Papá some work and he would be with him for sure."

"But that man doesn't live there anymore."

"Maybe he does."

The man gave Serafín the phone so he himself could hear the harsh voice: "That's right, I already told you, he went back to his village this past week, and good riddance." He hung up.

Serafín seemed to collapse completely, his arms hanging at his sides like a puppet whose strings had been cut.

"What are you going to do now?"

"I don't know," Serafín answered, looking at the worn tips of his shoes, with dust on them that seemed more than ever like dust from far, far away.

"Do you have anywhere to go?"

He shook his head, his firmly shut lips holding back a sob.

"How long has it been since you've eaten?"

"Yesterday . . ."

"Come on, let's go get something to eat."

◆ ◆ ◆ ◆

"Sometimes I heard your voice, Papá. I was going down the street and heard your voice so clearly, calling me: Serafín, Serafín. I turned around but you weren't there. It was just plain air, carrying your voice from wherever you might be. Sometimes I would hear your voice again, even stronger. I would crouch down low in order to hear it, but I didn't hear it anymore or heard it from far away, like the echo of your voice. I even hugged a man, I was so sure he was you, like in that game of tag when we would always bump into the one who wasn't it, the one who was just standing still, because the voice bounced around from the walls and corners. I was sure you were calling me, since maybe you heard I was already here in the city."

◆ ◆ ◆ ◆

They went to a small restaurant with neon lighting. The man crossed his long legs, lit a cigarette, and asked Serafín what he wanted to eat.

"Whatever you say."

"You're the one who's going to eat, not me. What do you want?"

"I don't know."

Under the very bright light, his misery was obvious.

"Some eggs and an orange juice?"

"Yes," he answered, without looking up.

When the waitress left, he seemed more at ease, but his eyes were still far away. There was a moment of silence and he slowly returned until he was there again and put the bag on the table.

"Put it on this chair," the man said, and was going to do it, but Serafín stopped him, holding it up against his chest and then placing it himself where the man had indicated. His blinking showed his distress.

"Yes," the man said lightly, smiling, "If you don't put it down yourself, you'll forget it."

"I have some things my mamá gave me."

Serafín felt desperation churning inside him, like a part of the sea within the walls of a port.

"You can cry if you want to, that always helps."

"No, no, I don't want to cry. I'm all right. Here, take it, look inside if you want to," and he held out the bag to him.

The man said he was not curious about seeing what was inside, but Serafín looked at him in such a way that he had to do it. He glanced into the bag.

"You have an apple here. Why haven't you eaten it?"

"I was waiting until I was hungrier."

He was going to return the bag, but Serafín stopped him.

"Look at the letter."

"What letter?"

"The one my mamá sent to my papá. It's at the very bottom."

The man had to take everything out before he came to the letter.

"Read it to me."

The man realized why Serafín had trusted him with the bag. It was the same trick as when he'd put the coin in his hand.

"You don't know how to read?"

"No."

The waitress brought a plate of fried eggs and beans with cheese sprinkled over them and a large orange juice.

"I think you saw her even though she wasn't right in front of you, like me . . . You saw her because you only saw what you had within you . . . The way your eyes were when you'd been drinking . . . How could you turn out to be so bad? . . . Pretty soon the rumor began and Serafín heard it . . ."

"Is your name Serafín?"

"Yes."

"Someone even said that you killed Cipriano to get his daughter. It's lucky no one cared or wanted to investigate it. What devil got into you? . . . Are you going to let us die of hunger? . . . If I don't matter to you, think of your children . . . Who else can help us? . . . By now not even Flaviano wants to lend us anything . . . Some days we eat nothing but tortillas . . . What are we going to do without you? . . ."

"Do you want me to go on?"

"Yes."

"Being alone has made me think at times about how you were before, when we first met, when Serafín was born and when you kissed me, you were kissing *me* . . . I saw you clearly in those days and I longed for your return . . . I don't know what it is, I don't know why . . . Now that you're far away, I can tell you that even if you were here, I wouldn't feel that way now . . . Now you're not like that and there's no way to make you go back in time . . . All I ask is that you send me some money with Serafín . . . The poor child has missed you more than you can imagine . . . Or get him a job, so he can send me something regularly . . ."

Serafín used a piece of bread to wipe up what was left of the egg yolk. The bread was black where he had touched it, but the man did not dare suggest that he go wash his hands.

"That's what it says."

"Thanks," and without the slightest change of expression, he took the letter and put it in the bag.

"I think we didn't really have to read it. You probably had an idea of what it said, didn't you?"

"More or less."

"To tell the truth, the one who annoys me most is your mamá. We're friends by now, so I can say that, can't I?"

The man noticed something passing across Serafín's eyes, moving as if among shadows in a forest, almost blindly. He asked him if he would like to have something else to eat and Serafín said, two more eggs and another orange juice. The man suggested a nice, juicy piece of meat, but Serafín insisted on some eggs exactly like the others.

"How are you going to get back?"

"I'm not going back."

"What are you going to do if you don't find your papá?"

"I'm going to find him."

"Where?"

"Around here."

And then, unhappily:

"He goes to cantinas a lot."

"So you're going to look for him in all the cantinas in the city?"

"I don't know."

With the back of his hand he wiped away an unexpected tear, and rubbed his eyes with both hands until the desire to cry went away.

"I'll give you the money to go back. Look, there's no place for you to stay. Nobody's going to help you, and the ones who may want to help you are the worst, because they'll only abuse you."

There was a long silence that seemed to form ice around them.

The man tried to look at him gently.

The waitress brought another plate of eggs and beans and another orange juice. When he had finished, he asked,

"Would you really give me the money to go back?"

"That's what I said."

"OK."

They left the restaurant to look for a taxi, which was not easy. When they found one, the man gave him some money and saw that he was seated in the back, his bag held before his chest like a shield. The man told the cab driver to take him to the bus station and here was a good tip; if possible, buy a ticket for him.

The man waved good-bye with a smile that was sideways because of the cigarette in the corner of his mouth. The cab stopped at the next corner and Serafín got out. He looked all around as if dazed and started running. The man was going to catch him, but it seemed absurd. What for?

13 **"Why did you deny** the talk about Cipriano's daughter if I was going to find her here? Were you ashamed to confess it in front of me? That my papá had another woman? Then why did you let me come, if in the end I wouldn't want to?"

◆ ◆ ◆ ◆

Serafín ran aimlessly, gasping for breath, sure by now the man could not catch him, but impelled by a strange, autonomous force. He tripped on the edge of a median and found himself seated on the grass, rubbing an elbow and gulping mouthfuls of air. The contents of the bag were scattered all around.

A woman came over.

"Little boy, did you hurt yourself very much? Why were you running so hard? Here, stand up so I can look at your arm."

She was a tall woman, very tall, dressed in white. Seen from below like that, foreshortened, in the blinding light of the sun, she seemed unreal, a product of the running and fall.

"No," Serafín said.

"Your things have fallen all over," and she made a motion as if about to bend over and pick them up.

"No, let them be," and he threw himself on the bag, covering it with his body and squirming around to hide the spilled contents.

When the sun hit him squarely on the neck, he realized the woman had left.

"Old busybody," he said between his teeth, hugging his things even closer.

Turning, he had only the sun above him, so low it seemed he could touch it. He opened his mouth but could not breathe. Cars were going past noisily on both sides, and he had the feeling of being on a raft on a full-flowing river. With his eyes on the sun and the deafening noise surrounding him, it was as if he were somewhere else, maybe on one of those days when he went to work with his papá. Had he looked at the sun like that then?

He watched a dove fly up to perch on a high cornice; there it was, concentrated in the clarity of the day. He wondered how old or how young it was and thought that a dove, young or old, could go wherever it wanted to go. It would always look at the world from above, and only when it got tired would it come down to see it from below.

He put his hands behind his neck. He was bothered only by the shadow of someone passing by too closely or an especially insistent horn.

"More likely it's a young dove."

♦   ♦   ♦   ♦

"I was talking to the devil, and that made her mad. She was praying, and I told her it was useless, that the God she was asking for things sent only grief to earth. To get out of poverty, you have to ask the devil. Then I yelled, O Satan, king of the underworld, if you exist, get us out of misery. She carried on like you've never seen, tried to scratch me and burst into tears. I couldn't help laughing, and she got worse, trembling, so your grandmother had to carry her to bed and cuddle her like a child. The way they looked at me, I preferred coming here to sleep."

"Don't you want me to bring you another cover?"

"No, this is enough. How was your mamá when you left the house?"

"Asleep, but my grandmother says she cried a lot because of what you said to her."

"I tell you it was only because of the part about the devil."

"Did you call to the real devil himself?"

"Yes, to the very one himself. The only one."

"Mamá is terribly afraid of the devil."

"Your mamá is afraid of everything."

"Do you think the devil really exists?"

"No, you can see we're as poor as ever."

"And if he really did exist? Imagine."

"By now, it doesn't matter. I'd ask him to give me some happiness for a while and pay later with my soul. Anyway, I can't be any more damned somewhere else than I am here on earth. And they say the fire puts the body to sleep and then you don't feel it so much."

"Could you do it?"

"There's nothing to that, understand? It's nothing but lies invented by women's fears. There are only clouds in the sky, and under the earth only more earth. And we'll keep on dragging our misery along until we reach the end of the rope. No one is going to come down to help us, and no one is going to give us a prize for having endured like burros."

"And what if there is a heaven?"

"If that's where your mamá and your grandmother are going, I'd rather stay here."

"You wouldn't want to be with them forever?"

"I wouldn't want to be with them at all."

"Mamá says when you're dying, you're going to repent of all the things you say about God and you'll go to heaven, too, and we'll all be very happy together forever."

"I can't even stand them here, where I can escape at times; imagine it there. They talk about jails made of clouds with guardian angels."

"Why can't you stand them?"

"Because they're so afraid and so ugly, that's why."

"She's my mamá. And my grandmother."

"Of course . . . but as soon as you and your brothers and sisters grow up a little more, I'm going—why wouldn't I leave?"

"Where will you go?"

"Wherever it is, it'll be far away from them. You should have seen the way they looked at me a little while ago. They're fed up, too, even if they don't say so. I'm going to a place where the people are different from the ones here. Where you don't have to pray and work from sunrise to sunset in order to get a little bit of bread."

"Do you still want to go to Mexico City?"

"One of these days I'm going to go there. They say it's hard, but at least there are opportunities. Here it's hard, and there's nothing. Everything is dry and it's going to get even drier."

"Can I go with you?"

"You're getting to be old enough to go by yourself. I left home when I was twelve and there was no way I was going back. My papá begged and begged, arguing that my mamá was crying for me a lot. But it's better for them to cry than to have you hung up by the neck. Go away and you won't be caught by one of these nagging women here, like your mamá and your grandmother. There's no way to deal with them, and if you think there is, it's worse, because you'll end up with poison inside you, just like me. Go by yourself. Why do you want to go with me?"

"Uncle Flaviano says it's better not to go."

"Because his wife already has him beaten down, and he always talks the way she wants him to. When he takes a couple of drinks, just see how she carries on. He says he doesn't drink because it's bad for his soul. What soul. It's his damn bitterness that comes out and wipes away the happiness. Who made him marry your Aunt María just so she could have him at her beck and call? What are they going to do with so much time together? She just takes advantage of him, and he lets her do it. That's all there is to it."

"Can I sleep here with you?"

"Yes, but bring your own cover. While you're at it you can see how your mamá is getting along."

"If I go, she won't let me come back."

"What a nuisance you are, too, you scamp. Come closer, you're going to die of cold, with this threadbare cover. Have a shot of tequila. It'll do you good."

14 **As soon as he saw her** behind the counter in the pharmacy, he knew she could help him. Short, very fair, with a face like a doll. He went in and told her what he needed, showing her the paper.

"You think your papá is still somewhere around here instead of going away with this man on the slip of paper or back to your village?"

"I'm sure, Señora."

"We can ask."

There were rosettes on her porcelain cheeks, just like a doll's. She dialed the number while Serafín's anxiety made his hands open and close as if he were squeezing limes.

"Yes, Señora . . . he just arrived in the city . . . a very good-looking boy, if you could just see him . . . with eyes to make you lose sleep." And she winked at Serafín. "He has the name and number of this man on a piece of paper . . . his Mamá sent him . . . yes, terrible . . . so many, Señora, so many . . . but, Holy Mother, what can we do? . . . if you'd be good enough . . . I'm not taking too much of your time? . . . of course, I understand, I'll wait."

She put her hand on the mouthpiece and turned to wink at Serafín.

"She's going to ask her servant."

Then she continued:

"Yes? . . . Oh, fine . . . don't tell me . . . how awful . . . that's the way these people are, you put your trust in them and look what happens . . . but it could have been worse . . . I appreciate it so much . . ."

She hung up the phone with a glowing smile and said,

"Look, the man on the paper really didn't go back to his village with his relatives. He went to jail because he stole some jewelry in that house. This woman says that, in fact, a few months ago he brought a friend to work for her as butler and gardener, but he had a woman with him, and she already had a woman working for her, so she couldn't take them both. This same servant later found out from the man on the paper that they had found work nearby, at a house in the same neighborhood, but she didn't know exactly which one. Would it be your papá who came with the woman?"

"Yes."

"But you still want to find him?"

"Yes."

"And if he doesn't want to go back with you? Now that he has another woman here."

"I have to give him the letter Mamá sent him. And I want to see him. I . . . since I left Aguichapan I've known about Cipriano's daughter."

"About who?"

"The girl he has with him is Cipriano's daughter."

His solemn air made her smile fade, but not disappear completely. She rounded her lips and firmed her voice, but the brilliance of her eyes and the rosettes in her cheeks betrayed her.

"Lord, Lord," she said and looked for a notebook and pencil in a drawer of the counter. "I'm going to write down the name of the neighborhood for you. Go over there to see what you find."

"Thank you, Señora."

She also gave him a hundred-peso bill, which Serafín carefully folded in half and put in the back pocket of his pants. As he was going out, he turned for a moment—why were the real good-byes always from a distance?—and she, elbows on the counter, gave him a wide smile, like a floating slice of a small moon.

◆ ◆ ◆ ◆

Papá was right; after feeling hungry for so long, you almost stopped feeling it. Although he'd said it about fire, not about hunger. But it must be the same, to die of hunger or burn up in flames. The body goes to sleep and turns into wood. It was difficult for him to walk, to lift one foot and then the other, as if he were on stilts. Since he had arrived in the neighborhood where he supposed his father was, he had not stopped walking. From one end to the other, in all directions, in front of the same stores, the same doors, the same cantinas (which he always looked into), the same people, even the same dogs.

But the days were passing and he wondered if he was going to last. As he wondered, the question made him dizzy. He looked up high, and that new fear returned to chill his bones.

How would it be to die?

So he preferred walking to sleeping. Even though sleep might overcome him anywhere, in front of the door of a house, or next to some tree.

One morning he was awakened by a kick in the ribs. It was a fat man, who said he did not like to have beggars sleeping outside his house. And although Serafín was already awake, he gave him another kick.

"You look like a dog, you filthy brat. Don't you have a home?"

Serafín picked up his sweater and bag clumsily as if he was really already dead and was picking up his own remains. When he stood up, he finally saw the fat man's eyes, like knives, and he ran away. The fat man might call a policeman, and then he would never find Papá.

◆　◆　◆　◆

"I knew you were staying around here, Papá. Something told me. That's why I started playing at walking with my eyes closed. I played it a lot in Aguichapan, and here it helped me with the fear. As if I were seeing more clearly. Feeling the wall or with my hands sticking out in front of me. Now I'm going to run into a man who is my Papá, I was thinking . . . And I ran into a whole lot of people and even a pole, but not you. Why, if you were also thinking of me, didn't we find each other?"

15 **He also enjoyed** looking at the city's stars. Because he slept so much in the street, under the open sky, he ended up learning them by heart, barely twinkling when they dared appear among the clouds and smoke. There was one he liked the most because it was the first one to appear. The most brilliant and the bluest. He watched it as if drinking it, excited to know one of the city's stars.

The rain, on the other hand, hurt him more than hunger. It plunged him into the earth, making him smaller, not letting him sleep and therefore making him remember his hunger more. One afternoon he walked under a fine rain that was like needles piercing his cheeks. And he had to sleep in wet clothes, curled up against a metal door that had a protective ledge above. The wet clothes made him feel he had been trapped in flypaper. He shivered and turned over on the concrete, using his sweater as a pillow.

Actually he had never liked rain, and thunder even less. It was because once when it was raining hard, Papá had come home infuriated to complain to Mamá about something they'd said about her in the village. Something from when they did not even know each other and she had another boyfriend. Papá yelled at her to wake up and then they began quarreling.

"Yes, I liked him a lot. So?"

"What did he do to you? What else did he do? Where? Tell me or . . ."

Within the bluish darkness, the blow was swallowed by the noise of the storm, like Mamá's smothered moan and Papá's yelling.

"You knew about him . . . Why are you doing this now?"

"How did he do it to you? Tell me. Here? This way? Or harder?"

"The children are going to hear us, Román. No."

"This way?"

In a moment a flash of lightning showed Serafín his papá's eyes, like rubber balls. Then they were embracing and moving around in the bed, with Mama's moans each time more smothered and flat, guttural, as the cover over them formed the crest of a dark, throbbing wave.

So the nights when it rained were longer. Some of them did not ever stop because it kept on raining after dawn, making day into night. Not even the daylight could calm the bitterness of the rain that was born at night. It was different if it started raining when it was already day, and there was no thunder. A rain that started in the afternoon had the advantage of carrying some of the light left from morning, so the bitterness did not come until later. Some-times it didn't come at all if the rain stopped early.

◆ ◆ ◆ ◆

Alma found him on one of those nights when he slept wherever he was. Wondering how they could let a child sleep like that, lying right in the street, she looked at him and recognized Serafín. She squatted down and moved his shoulder.

Although he was sitting up, it was as if Serafín were still dream-ing, with a familiar face in front of him. Who was it? And really, to see the face of a person he knew in those circumstances seemed to sink him even deeper into the dream. Where did he come from? And where did she come from? He rubbed his eyelids and looked at Alma bleary-eyed.

"Don't you remember me? I'm Alma, Cipriano's daughter. Ci-priano. You do remember Cipriano, don't you?"

He stretched out his hand and felt her as if he were feeling the dream itself.

"I think you saw her even though she wasn't right in front of you, like me . . . You saw her because you only saw what you had within you . . . Pretty soon the rumor began going around and Serafín heard it . . . Someone even said that you killed Cipriano to get his daughter . . ."

"What are you doing here?"

"I went to sleep."

"But why here?"

"Because I got so sleepy. I've walked all over these streets look-ing for my papá. Is he with you?"

Alma was looking at him as if she had caught Serafín's feeling of being deeper and deeper into a dream.

"He was, but he's gone. We were living together in a house near here. I still live there."

She took his hand and made him stand up. She took him through the fog along streets Serafín knew by heart.

"And it's been so cold, in the middle of December, Serafín," and she pressed his hand as if trying to give warmth to his whole body.

"Where did my papá go?"

"Don't worry, it's near here. In this same neighborhood. But he has a business going. Let's get you something to eat and I'll tell you about it."

They turned into a street edged with lines of dwarf trees and soon there was the house. A poplar covered with frost caught the pale light from the distant streetlight on the corner. The house had a rusty railing finished off with arrow tips and a garden with symmetrical trees trimmed as if by scissors. So this was the house, Serafín thought, looking at it with eyes that were now wide-awake; he had passed in front of it so many times. Alma took a single key out of her apron pocket and opened the door quietly.

"We have to be very quiet because the people who live here go to bed at nine o'clock and any little noise will wake them up."

They entered through a garage with two cars like hearses and went to the rear of the house. The room was tiny, with a cot, a chair, and some rough shelves for clothing. On the cot there was a small, yellowed, blurred photograph (obviously cut from a larger one) of a very thin man with white hair and a listless smile.

"It's Cipriano, my papá. You remember my papá, don't you, Serafín?"

16 **It was Cipriano** who realized how the people were exploited. One morning anger overwhelmed him and he began talking to rouse them. How hard do you work, and how much money do you make, and how are you doing at selling corn? Do you realize how much of your life is used up growing corn? Look at how prices have gone up. Add it up. He saw injustice in all of it, this Cipriano. They're taking advantage of you, sucker. Don't you see? What do they offer you and what do they pay? In the cantina they turned their back on him because he would just make their drinks bitter, especially the ones who had just arrived and were not drunk enough yet.

But he did draw people to him, so much so that one night a crowd of at least half the village gathered outside his house. They even brought infants, so they could hear those words that were going to be repeated later on, like echoes.

He invited them one by one.

"On Sunday, after the seven o'clock Mass, I'm going to talk about your problem here in my house. Everyone's problem. But since I'm going to talk especially about you, it's better to have you come."

They said when the Municipal President found out about it, he only shrugged his shoulders and clicked his tongue.

"No one's going to touch him," he said. "No one will go."

But they did go, many of them.

Cipriano was tall and tough, and that helped him when he spoke in public. He had presence, as they say. He lived in the outskirts of the village, in a house of wood that he himself had built. He knew how to build, cultivate the land, and weave sombreros. Always alone, except for his daughter, and with a pile of books that he had been given here and there over a long period of time. They even said he had written some articles under another name occasionally for a newspaper in Mexico City, but that was never confirmed.

They also said his daughter was not his, but belonged to a poor prostitute, who was beaten to death by a bunch of policemen because she had rejected one of them. Cipriano, who for some strange reason knew her, claimed her body and the child. He buried the woman and was left with the child, who was then already a good ten years old and already giving promise of being as pretty as she would be later on.

◆　◆　◆　◆

Serafín remembered one night when he and his papá went to visit Cipriano. He was weaving one of the sombreros that his daughter would later sell in the market. He had finished the crown and was starting on the brim, adding new fibers.

"Working with your hands is the best way to rest from the books," he told them agreeably, but without real pleasure in seeing them. He invited them in to sit down and went on with his work.

"I can't offer you any tequila because I don't have any," he apologized.

"I imagined that, so I brought a little," Serafín's papá said, taking a bottle out of his knapsack and putting it on the table, which changed Cipriano's forced pleasantness into open disgust.

"Well, you'll drink it alone because I don't drink," he said dryly.

"If it doesn't bother you . . ."

"Even if it does bother me, it can't be helped."

But then, as if he felt sorry because he had been abrupt, which was not usual with him, he said,

"If you'd like something to eat, I have tortas with *nopal* and *frijoles*. How about you, Serafín?"

"Thanks, we've already eaten," his papá said quickly, cutting off the acceptance in Serafín's mouth.

The light wavered outward from a large tallow candle on a ledge. In a corner there was a straw sleeping mat with unraveled edges, and nearby a hammock where Cipriano's daughter was swinging. It was there Serafín got to know her although he did not see her face clearly as she went back and forth.

"How come you're getting the people together on Sunday, Cipriano?"

"You'll see."

"Man, give us a hint," and Papá offered the bottle of tequila again, which Cipriano again rejected.

"It's the time for sacrifice."

"What kind of sacrifice?"

Cipriano's eyes were on his work as he used a needle to tear the palm leaf into thin fibers.

"You're really stubborn, Román. You can't wait until tomorrow? Or did you come to set something up for a friend?" His eyes locked briefly into Papá's, who had to turn his away and look at the bottle of tequila. "Don't have anything to do with the people in power, Román. They always demand more than they give."

"What do I have to do with that? If anyone here has stood up to the people from the government, I'm the one. I came to see if I could help you, but if you don't trust me, that's the end of it."

"I only said it just in case. We have to distrust even our own shadows. If I tell you anything, you'll spread it around, even without meaning any harm, and by tomorrow, everyone will know and it will have already fizzled. So isn't it better to keep quiet?"

"All right."

"Don't be annoyed. Excuse me if I misjudged you, but we're dealing with the destiny of Aguichapan and lots more. If you really want to help, tomorrow you'll have more than enough opportunities."

"Whatever you propose, you know I'll pull with you, Cipriano. So it hurt me that you took me for a squealer."

"My plan is up here," Cipriano said, touching his forehead lightly. "It's the result of my whole life and all I've read. If someone in the government finds out what it is, they will come and kill me. But that's not important; the tragedy would be if it should frustrate the possibility of salvation for all."

"If it's like that, forgive me for coming here to pester you."

"Look, if my own mamá on her death bed asked me, I would not tell her, and that says it all."

"And I tell you that you can count on me for anything that will help me get out of this dark hole I'm stuck in."

More than anything else, Serafín remembered Cipriano's bony hands, with veins standing out in very dark blue: veritable rivers with branches, tributaries, deltas.

◆　◆　◆　◆

And in order to say what he did not want to talk about earlier, Cipriano called the people together the following night. There was a dull buzz of voices until he appeared on top of a wooden bench, thinner and with all of his nerves taut, like guitar strings. Outside the house he put pine torches; burning and spitting with the odor of resin, they created a strange atmosphere, both festive and mysterious. He stopped from time to time for brief gulps of air, which then came out as living words. He asked the same questions as always, but to all of them together and also as if to each one, making it seem like a doubly strong interrogation. What were they doing there? Who were they working for? Why believe in God if it meant letting their children die of hunger or, in most cases, grow up hungry, without education, condemned to be slaves for life, as they themselves were. Yes, slaves: you have to call things what they are. How many hours did they work every day? And why, for whom? Of the promises made, how many have been kept? And they should look at their calloused hands, yes, they should look at their hands, worn and tired from working the earth. And to feed whom? How much of what they raised was for them, for their children? Did they know that in the large cities there were people who made great fortunes they could live on without working for the rest of their lives, just from selling again what they grew?

And suddenly he was quiet, which intensified what he had said, letting the words float by themselves around the people for a while. Then someone raised a long forefinger and asked:

"And what are we going to do to change things, Cipriano? You haven't told us that."

"Be ready for the sacrifice."

And again the silence, like the hum of bees frightened by smoke.

"More sacrifices?" someone dared ask. Cipriano definitely expected it because he said emphatically:

"The true sacrifice."

"Which, Cipriano, which one?" several people asked at the same time.

"The one of thinking first of others instead of ourselves."

The wind fought with the flames from the pine torches.

"Come on, spit it out without so much blahblahblah," someone in the back of the group yelled.

"A hunger strike. But a serious hunger strike, until its final consequences. And not here, but in Mexico City itself, and in front of the President of the Republic, in the middle of the Zócalo. Yes, sir! We'll see who will keep us from dying of hunger, right there in the center of injustice, as some say! We'll see if they can stifle our silent scream! If we have only our poor lives to save our children, we'll give them!"

That was when applause rained down on Cipriano, along with cries and insults. One woman carrying an infant even dug her elbow into her husband's side because he applauded.

"You're a madman!"

"Long live Cipriano! I'm going with him!"

124

"We'd better arm ourselves and arrive shooting!"

"In that case our sacrifice would be futile," Cipriano said. "How long would it take them to finish us off with the arms they have? The way it is, they're going to have to endure our long agony."

"But what's the point?"

"So they'll listen to us. So they'll hear our lament and the lament of the ones that came before us and the lament of the ones who will come after us. So they'll find out how deep our pain is. Who hears us here? Nobody. But they'll listen to death. I'd like to see what the newspapers say when hundreds of humble men from the country begin dying of hunger in the very center of the city. Even the tourists and the foreign newspapers will talk about us."

"What are we going to ask for?"

"Nothing. And everything. Our protest will make them wake up once and for all."

"They'll put us in jail!"

"If there are enough of us, no."

"You're really crazy, Cipriano."

"Why continue life in this filth? If it falls to us to be martyrs, well, so be it."

"Yes, yes!"

"Most of us are as damned as if we had already died. Isn't it better to offer to humanity what little we have left?"

"What if we rot in the Zócalo and they don't pay any attention to us or give our children anything?"

"It's because of doubts like those that we're the way we are! Justice will be established in the land of men of faith, not fearful men."

"Yes, yes. We have to help establish justice!"

"But our children will be abandoned!"

"Can they be more abandoned than they are now, with us or without us? Have you seen the future before them, even if we live a hundred years? Ask yourselves and then see if it's worth the sacrifice to offer them another world, not only to our children but to everyone's children."

"Yeah, by dying in the Zócalo we're going to change the world? Don't kid yourself, Cipriano!"

"Our sacrifice is just a seed, but it will give fruit that will have countless seeds."

"If people start to commit suicide, there won't be anyone left in the world."

"Or it'll change the situation for the ones who are left. In them perhaps we'll see the divine light."

"How will we go?"

"On foot. That way the newspapers will start talking about us before we get there."

The women gathered to the side in a group, talking anxiously. A really old man said he couldn't survive the trip on foot, would they let him go on the bus even if it was just to die, but they decided unanimously they should go together or not go at all. They began to disperse with a dull buzz of voices, and a few wrote their names on a list that Serafín's papá offered to carry around. Not many, but a good forty. The night closed in again when Cipriano, now alone, put out the torches and went into his house.

17 **When the time came,** only thirty of those forty decided to go. They were a small group of men waving good-bye, like a squad of unhappy recruits—perhaps because from the beginning they were imagining how they were going to suffer hunger later. Cipriano in front, guiding them, gesturing and talking constantly, throwing out the words he had kept to himself during his years of silence.

Some people from the village followed them for one section of the highway, delaying the farewell. They turned around, smiled, and kept on waving good-bye until suddenly they disappeared, as if the horizon had swallowed them.

Some came back the following day: they could not stand the hunger or fatigue or missing the family, or a friend persuaded them that it was an absurd pilgrimage. Others were returning later (among them Serafín's papá), for the same reasons or because, so they said, when arriving in the city, they left the group for a moment and did not find them again. Some never came back.

"And So-and-so?"

"I don't know, I lost him on the road. I think he went into a village we passed by and hasn't left yet."

Or:

"I don't know where he went in the city. He might even have found some work."

They returned in small groups of three and four, heads down, their faces showing more shame (one confessed he had eaten something on the road) than hunger. Or afraid that their wives would receive them coldly, or worse, with fury. At least one had to hit his wife to settle her down. As if they weren't the ones who were returning from a long march, and (almost) without eating.

"Did they get to the Zócalo?"

"Very few. Seven of us got to the city, and as I recall, even before reaching the Zócalo, two preferred to look around the city a little because there are so many attractions, and we never saw them again. Another got drunk from a jug he bought on the way . . . and I can't remember what happened to another one."

Cipriano was in the last group of four returning to Aguichapan. And he was a changed Cipriano. Or better said, he was the old Cipriano, who did not talk or have nerves as taut as guitar strings. So he went right to his house with his daughter (who had stayed with a kind widow) and did not come out again, except to get water or cut firewood. He sent his daughter to buy food or sell sombreros in the village, and she hardly spoke.

◆ ◆ ◆ ◆

The three who were with Cipriano until the end told what happened. They contradicted each other but agreed more or less on the important part. They got to the Zócalo early one cold morning, dragging their swollen, lacerated feet—after they came to the first lights on the highway, Cipriano insisted that the reporters would be more impressed if they saw them barefooted—dying of hunger and thirst but with the happiness of finally reaching their goal. The large cloth held on high was like a flag with red letters: "LET DEATH SPEAK FOR US." They had crossed the city like silent shadows, hardly touching the cement with their bare feet, and with the sunrise and beginning hubbub, they were already seated in the very center of the Zócalo, looking toward the National Palace. Some curious people came near them (especially those coming from the Metro), and some who were really interested advised them to leave because the government had prohibited any kind of demonstration and would beat the hell out of them.

With the sun climbing, a group of policemen arrived and asked them what they were doing, but they did not answer. Because the policemen persisted, Cipriano pointed to the cloth and said:

"Can't you read? We came to starve to death."

"Nobody can starve to death here. Come on, you have to do it somewhere else. Demonstrations and protests are forbidden here."

Cipriano was right at the beginning. If there had been many of them, they could not have moved them so easily. But with only four, they could do whatever they wanted. A hit here, another there, in the kidneys, a kick in the ribs, a club to the head. They took away the cloth and ripped it up. Cipriano looked desperately for a reporter to write up the event, take pictures. But perhaps because it was so early, none appeared. Only a well-dressed lady who waved her hands in the faces of the policemen:

"Don't hit them, you brutes. They're not hurting anyone."

"They're blocking the public road."

"They're not blocking anything. It would be better for you to side with them."

But by pulling and hitting they got rid of the first one. And then it was easier with the second and third. Cipriano was the only one they could not move. It seemed he had put down roots, making himself part of the concrete he was sitting on, becoming concrete himself. He only blinked at their blows, and swayed like a tree in a storm.

"Hey, leave this one here. No one's paying any attention to him."

So they left him. The other three started on the road home with sore bodies, but even sorer hearts, because they had failed at the very end. They got something to eat and drink with some pesos one of them had. Before leaving the city, with the moon already above, they agreed they could not leave Cipriano there. What was the point? By himself? He was going to die of hunger and no one would pay attention. Also, if he gave up, he had no money to buy anything to eat.

◆　◆　◆　◆

When they got back to the Zócalo, the traffic had diminished and there were fewer people entering and leaving the Metro. Cipriano was seated with his legs crossed, exactly as they had left him, as if he were meditating in the light of the moon, perhaps a little more bent over, sinking into himself, beginning to die. People passed by him, hardly seeing him, perhaps thinking him drunk. Without the banner, who could imagine what he intended.

"Come, Cipriano. Why are you staying here by yourself?"

"Better to work at home for the people."

"As a teacher you would do more good than dying here alone."

"Who's going to know about it?"

"We've failed, can't be helped. You're humble because you've read a lot, and you can recognize it."

"You're going to die in vain. An ambulance will come and who knows where they'll bury you. Think of your daughter, so beautiful and young. They still pay attention to you, but how many reporters came up to ask you questions? The truth is, none. You see?"

Then Cipriano got up as decisively as he had sat down, sighed deeply, and said, let's go. They say he uttered not one word more on the way home. He ate a piece of bread with sardines and took a long drink of beer. On the highway he accepted a ride on a bus that offered to take them for free. His eyes were unfocused and he was bent over as if he were still part of the concrete, but he got on, which was the important thing—to rescue him from that useless death.

They said that the following morning, before entering the village, Cipriano stopped on a high promontory with yellow underbrush, where you could see the whole village. He went into the underbrush to see the village better, to take it all in. The sun silvered the whitewashed houses. Here and there the resignation of the animals, the banks of mist spreading and mingling with the timid smoke issuing from the chimneys, some men working the hot mortar, some children coming out of their houses and huts as if to create the world. Cipriano looked at all of them from above, the best place to see, and said only:

"To hell with all of it."

It was the last thing they heard him say until the day he died.

18 **Six long months passed,** during which the village finally became normal again, after the gossip and frustrated emotion. Until one morning someone told Serafín's papá that Cipriano was bleeding badly because he had been shot in the leg and no one wanted to help him, not even the doctor.

Cipriano was already dying when Serafín's papá arrived. His profile was sharper than ever, and he seemed to be burning up because he could not get enough air into his body. Serafín's papá remembered the day when Cipriano spoke to them outside his house. Why did his face look the same way it had that night?

And that was when he entrusted his daughter, Alma, to him.

"Don't let her become a whore, Román. Anything but that. Find her a good man . . . She's such a nice young woman."

Also he asked to be buried at the foot of his jacaranda tree. And he wanted his house to be burned so no trace of his books would remain. Serafín's papá did bury him at the foot of his jacaranda tree, but was afraid to burn the house without written permission from the deceased.

It was never known who killed him, but the gossips in the town were sure it was one of the women who'd lost her husband in the pilgrimage. Or one of the men, resentful because his wife would not let him in the house when he got back. Others said the Municipal President ordered that he be killed just because he had caused such trouble in the past months. But it was hard to imagine someone would hide his resentment for months and then show it when everything was quiet, although who knows. Anyway, since it did not matter to anyone, no investigation was made.

◆　◆　◆　◆

And now here was his daughter, Alma, more grown-up with her curvy hips. She had tawny skin and eyes that changed from softest gray to softest aquamarine. She had taken off the dirty apron and the loose white dress, revealing her shapely legs. She was carrying a tray with steaming broth, a roll, and a glass of milk.

She put the tray on the bed and Serafín moved toward it trembling, his hunger suddenly concentrated in the flavor of his saliva. However, in spite of having it in front of him, within reach of his hand, the food seemed very far away. Sleepiness, hunger itself, deranged him, numbing his will and the tips of his fingers.

"It's going to get cold, better eat it right away," Alma said in her gentle voice, looking at him with a smile through a lock of dark chestnut hair falling over her eyes.

The light from the bulb was glaring heavily on everything.

Then Serafín stretched out a hand that broke the block of ice surrounding him and picked up the roll. He bit into it as if tearing off a piece of hard meat, and swallowed it dry because his saliva had dried up.

"You look very pale, Serafín."

The broth scalded his tongue like a river of fire, but he swallowed it quickly. And since the milk was very cold, it seemed to him he heard his stomach sizzling, like red hot metal plunged into water. The chicken, on the other hand, did not settle anywhere, but stayed in his esophagus, swelling there.

"My God, Serafín, what is happening to you?"

He put his hands on his stomach and started writhing. The tray nearly fell over on the cot, but Alma rescued it in time.

"I feel as if I have a ball here in my chest."

"A ball?"

"Like the food is making a ball inside me here."

"Oh, my God, don't get sick, then what would we do?"

But Serafín barely got his head clear of the cot before vomiting everything he had eaten. From that moment on everything was confused, as if he had climbed on an unsteady kite and could see what was happening in the room. Alma's soft hands stroking his neck, the cotton with alcohol, the camomile tea (which he also threw up immediately, in an arch), and the woman in a robe who suddenly appeared in the doorway.

"Who is this child?"

Her messed-up hair and the way she showed her teeth gave her face a look both pathetic and terrible.

"He's the son of my husband, Señora. By his first wife."

"Why did you bring him here without telling me?"

"I found him in the street a few moments ago. He was asleep on the sidewalk. I didn't want to awaken you, Señora."

"What happened to him?"

"I gave him a little broth and he vomited everything. Probably because he hasn't eaten for several days."

"He's very pale. Greenish. He should see a doctor early tomorrow."

She went toward the cot and stretched out a hand that looked like a menacing claw to Serafín, who fell back against the wall.

"What were you doing around here, child?"

Serafín did not answer, but continued looking at her with the eyes of a small, trapped animal. He pushed up against the wall as if longing to get through to the other side.

"He came to find his father, Señora. Tomorrow I'll take him there."

"Poor children. So you can see what you're mixed up in. With those irresponsible men all of you choose as fathers of your children. Give him some tea."

"I've already done that, but he vomited it also."

"Then let him rest his stomach and see a doctor tomorrow. He's shivering, put more covers on him. Come with me, I'll give you another blanket."

"We're all right this way, Señora. I'll put some of my clothes on top of him. Don't go to any trouble. You have to get up early tomorrow."

"Clean up all of this. It stinks."

As soon as the woman left, Serafín sat up on the cot, his eyes bright, revived.

"Are you my Papá's new wife?"

"No, but we're going to have a child," Alma answered while she mopped up the floor.

"A child? Why?"

"Well . . . you know, because we love each other. I became his woman the day my papá died."

"Do you have the address where he is now?"

"I know where it is. It's a store a few blocks from here. He made friends with the owner, an old woman who lives alone with her children. He works with her now because he had trouble with the owner here."

"Have you gone to see him?"

"Only once. He doesn't want me to go there. He says it's better for him to come here."

"How long has it been since he came here?"

"A couple of weeks. But he has to stay there, or he would have told me. I'm telling you, he has a lot of work to do."

"OK, write down the address for me."

"Now? It would be better tomorrow."

"Please."

"We're going to sleep now. You're sick."

"But I can't sleep until I see the address written down. Please?"

"Well, just so you can satisfy your curiosity."

From one of the shelves, under a blouse and some underwear messily stuffed in, she took down some pieces of paper and wrote the name of a street and a number.

"Why written, Serafín?"

"I like writing."

"Do you know how to read?"

"No, but I like it anyway."

Serafín looked at the paper, dazzled. Here was his Papá. Going there meant he could be with him, reclaim him, embrace him. Some marks he could not understand, but finally a map of the treasure so long sought.

"I'm going to find him right now."

And saying it made him angry with himself for the moments when he doubted, or felt afraid, or was sad or tired or sleepy.

◆　◆　◆　◆

"Where did that moan come from, Mamá?"

"What moan, child? You're just hearing things in your dreams, and think you're really hearing them. Go to sleep."

"But listen, you can hear it clearly."

"It must be an abandoned lamb bleating, but we can't do anything about it now. Tomorrow we'll see."

"I can't sleep while I hear it, Mamá."

"I'm telling you to sleep. You have to make believe you don't hear it."

"But I do hear it."

"Be quiet and let me sleep."

19

"**You're crazy, Serafín.** It's almost midnight."

"That doesn't matter. I'll get there and wake him up. I'll tell him we couldn't sleep because of thinking so much about him. Just imagine. After so much time without seeing me."

Alma's eyes almost closed as she thought about it. Of course, it was more likely to find him there now than tomorrow during the day, and since it was so close . . . Also, the Señora wanted Serafín to see a doctor. What if he was sick and had to spend all day in bed? They might even put him in the hospital. God knows she did not want that, but with the doctors in the city, you never knew.

"How do you feel?"

"I'm fine now. Look, I can even stand up," and he jumped to his feet, opened his hands, and smiled with a smile that made up for the lack of color in his cheeks.

"I can even sing: Tra-la-la . . ."

To Alma he seemed grotesque standing there in his drill pants with patches and mending on the knees, and more mending on top of the patches; his shoes covered with that dust from far away; his faded blue sweater, very dirty, the sleeves unraveled; his body shapeless, as if he were about to lose what body he had left under his clothes. With arms open like that he looked like a tiny scarecrow, a small figure comically crucified.

"Tra-la-la . . ."

"Enough, Serafín!"

"Tra-la-la" and he jumped a little, putting his heels together.

"Be quiet, the Señora is going to hear you!" but she could not keep from smiling, captured by that secret strength that shone through all the shadows. "I'm going to write a letter to your papá. I've been wanting to write to him. Tell him he can come back here whenever he wants to, the Señor has already forgiven him."

When she finished the letter, Alma's eyes were a brighter green. She went to the front door with Serafín on her tiptoes, hardly touching things, as if caressing them, and there she decided, "I'll walk a few blocks with you. I hope the Señora doesn't catch me."

She stopped when they got to a boulevard with a median and palm trees.

"I'll go back now. At the next street, turn to the left. Do you know which way is left? That's it. Then find number ninety-seven. It's very close. I wrote it on the paper. If you see someone, ask them. Don't get lost."

But Serafín was in such a hurry, he did not hear her final words. He waved good-bye and started running, wrapped in the cloud of vapor that came out of his mouth.

As he ran, he felt the cold of the night like a huge wave suspended over him, crowned by a misty foam, that lowered very slowly and from one moment to another burst just at his side. He had to run faster, to get out of the clutch of the intense cold . . .

◆ ◆ ◆ ◆

"The worst thing, Serafín, is to despair, give in to the weight of fatigue, or the discomfort in your stomach, or the urge to curl up in some doorway, like a dog—that's what they've called you, filthy brat, you look like a dog. Would it matter to you now if your body were allowed to collapse, your muscles to relax, your eyes to close? In any old corner or at the foot of one of those palm trees in the middle of the street, which at this hour casts a shadow as if to ward off the terrors of the night. You know it, but today is not like any other day and you have to keep yourself going because you're finally going to see your papá. Pull yourself together. Tell yourself it's not so cold. You've always been good at thinking things are not what they seem."

"But why is the cold hurting me more today? I've been walking here for so many nights, and it never hit me so hard."

"It's the emotion, Serafín, that makes the body weak. And on top of your own, you're carrying my feelings, which are no less than yours."

"You knew I was going to see Papá today?"

"I've known everything along with you. At times I was afraid you wouldn't be able to see him."

"Why didn't you answer me? I talked and talked to you, and you didn't answer me."

"Don't carry me with you all the time, Serafín. Me, with all my troubles, my complaints. Why do you want to carry me along with you? Someday I'm going to die and if you're used to carrying me inside you, you won't let me go. I'm no use to you. I'm just a nuisance. And when I'm already dead, you won't let me rest. What the dead need is rest."

"Is that why you didn't want me to keep on talking to my grandmother?"

"That's why. The poor thing didn't recover her soul completely; she left part of it here with us and came back to look for it."

"What did you tell her?"

"To go on. It was going to hurt you to spend so much time with the dead. You were very little, and I was worried. So I told her to go, even though she had to continue her way with an incomplete soul."

"And why are you talking to me now, Mamá?"

"Because I'm really afraid for you. You don't know how much I've regretted sending you. But also I wanted you to see your papá. To find out once and for all if he still loved us."

"But you're alive, aren't you, Mamá?"

"Yes, Serafín, I'm alive and waiting for you."

◆　◆　◆　◆

He knocked timidly on the metal security curtain, but the only response was the distant barking of a dog.

The night was growing deeper, finally hiding the stars, covering them with cold.

He kept knocking on the metal curtain harder and harder until his knuckles could no longer stand it, with the cold spreading deeper as he waited. He turned his face down and felt a hot tear. A single, unexpected tear. Papá, he said in a low voice.

Then the metal curtain began to go up.

It was as if the curtain was lifting on a long-expected dream.

There was Papá, standing in the night, so overwhelming Serafín had to step back and clutch his bag against his chest.

"What are you doing here?" Papá asked while pulling up the zipper on his denim pants.

"I came to find you."

"How did you know I was here?"

"Alma told me."

"Alma?"

"Yes, Alma."

"And how did you find her?"

"She saw me in the street. I was looking for you around here. Mamá gave me a telephone number to call you, but you weren't there anymore. So they told me to look for you around here."

"Come on in."

They went in, and Papá turned on the light and lowered the metal curtain. The small shop had a rickety showcase and a rack with five shelves. The meagerness of the stock—jars of fruit preserves or honey, cigarettes, matches, bags of brown sugar, bunches of aromatic herbs, candies inside the showcase—indicated a business that was just starting out or not very prosperous. Tapers and votive candles were hanging from nails. A door at the back was half open.

Looking stubborn, Serafín's papá went to sit on a wooden bench and leaned his elbows on the showcase, wearing the red and blue plaid shirt that Serafín remembered seeing in Aguichapan.

"Your Mamá told you to come to look for me?"

"Yes, she wanted to know if you're going to come back to us someday."

"Did she give you some money?"

"Very little. Just enough for the bus fare and a little more. It was gone soon."

"Who would have thought."

"She sent you this letter."

Serafín's papá trembled angrily, as if the words he was reading were making him come apart. At the end he gave a nervous laugh, which contrasted with the look of fury in his eyes. "Your mamá is crazy. You see how crazy she is? You see why I can't live with her anymore? You see why anything is preferable to living with her? You see why I was telling you I was about to go crazy if I stayed with her? You see why I preferred to come to the city to look for something else? Anything except her."

He leaned back on the bench and opened his hands to Serafín, as if to show his unhappiness, his helplessness.

Serafín recovered the letter abandoned on the showcase. He put it in his bag and took out the one from Alma.

"Alma also sent you a letter."

His Papá took it with his fingers like burning tongs. Now his lips showed something like shame. A fly was hovering and buzzing around between the glasses of honey.

"They can really screw you."

"Are you living here?"

"Yes, with the owner of the store and her children. She's an older widow and has been nicer to me than you could imagine."

"Could I go in there?" Serafín pointed to the partly opened door. "What for?"

"To go to the bathroom. And you can read the letter from Alma, OK?"

"But don't make any noise. One of the children has been kind of sick."

As Serafín went in, he had the feeling that started when he heard the metal curtain going up. A feeling he should experience completely, that began when he left Aguichapan. Or maybe before. Maybe the night when his papá left home. Or possibly even earlier.

The time of his grandmother's terror. Or when the rainy nights started to frighten him. Something that embedded itself within him like a fundamental doubt, ever since his first visions of the world.

The orange light from the store barely reached the surprised faces. The woman, the boy, and the girl squeezed together like a single three-headed body, in the two joined beds, with the cover pulled up to their chests. What were they afraid of? Of him, of Serafín? How would he look to them from their hiding place in the bed? And who were they?

20 **"There are two children, Mamá.** A boy about my age and a younger girl. And a really skinny woman. At least to me she seems very thin, worn out. Or is the light fooling me?"

"Get out of there, Serafín."

"Would Papá rather be with them than with us?"

"Hurry, Serafín, get out of there."

◆ ◆ ◆ ◆

"I'm going to the bathroom, Señora."

But the woman did not answer; she only pulled the edge of the sheet a little higher, up to her bony neck, perhaps afraid of covering her face completely.

"Is that the door to the bathroom?"

Serafín heard a tiny voice hardly breaking the silence, probably from the boy.

"Yes, it's there, over there."

Groping his way through things, he dodged chairs, tables, and a pile of boxes to reach the door. He left the door ajar and managed to urinate in the dimness. If they heard him, so what. He felt a kind of tear in the thin membrane of sentiment that had motivated him until then. In his eyes flickered the fear of what he had sensed in his inmost being, there, in complete darkness.

"Hurry, Serafín, get out of that place."

He tore the letter from Mamá to Papá into as many bits as possible and threw them into the toilet.

Going back, he was guided by the beam of light, brighter when looking right at it. It seemed like the exit to a labyrinth in spite of the nearness of the door. He no longer paid attention to the shadows of the beds and wall; now he himself was avoiding the faces of the woman and the children. He tripped over a box and almost fell to the floor, and heard a small soprano voice:

"Be careful, Serafín."

"I heard him clearly call me by my name. What do they know about me, or you, or my brothers and sisters? What has Papá told them?"

And the small voice, that came from the darkest part of the room, impossible to place at that moment, added:

"There are some other boxes farther along."

"Yes . . ." he was going to say thanks, but the word stayed in his mouth, changing into a light croak.

He emerged into the light and blinked.

"Hurry."

Papá was sitting bent over on the bench under the glare of harsh light, his chin in his hand and his eyes looking away, with a newly opened bottle of tequila at his side, which Serafín thought he was imagining or dreaming until Papá gave it life by lifting it with his free hand, his position unchanged, holding it to his lips.

"Papá, I'm leaving now."

There was a silence during which the light became clearer along with the wavering buzz of a fly moving around among the glasses of honey.

"Serafín, my son," Papá finally said, swinging the bottle like a pendulum, hypnotizing himself. "If you only knew the situation I'm in. I've even had to rob gas tank caps from cars . . . But I saved this money . . . I've been saving it for a while to send to your mamá, and now you can take whatever you need to return and to buy something for yourself and something for your brothers and sisters . . . It's not much, five thousand pesos, but I don't have any more . . . You understand, don't you?"

"Hurry."

"Papá, I'm going now. Really."

"Put that money away carefully."

Serafín obeyed and begged his papá to let him leave. But his papá stood up and, taking him by the hand, told him to spend that night there whether he wanted to or not. Outside it was very cold and tomorrow he himself would take him to the bus station. Also, he was going to send a letter to Mamá. Serafín saw himself taken helplessly to the room, but as soon as he felt the darkness in his face, he stopped.

"No, please, Papá."

"No, what?"

"I don't want to sleep with them. Please."

"Hurry."

"Don't be stubborn, Serafín. It's only one night. Tomorrow you're going back to Aguichapan."

"Please."

"Hurry."

"Then where are you going to go?" he said, raising his voice, hitting Serafín with it.

"I'm going to Alma's. She's waiting for me. It's very close."

"It's very cold, you know."

"Don't make me sleep with them, Papá. I'm begging you."

"Go on then! You'd think they smelled bad."

"Can you imagine sleeping with them, Serafín?"

"I just don't want to."

"Is that what you came from Aguichapan for?"

"I'm going now. I'll come back tomorrow."

"But you'll spend tonight here."

"No," and he slipped his hand free, regretfully.

"Look, I already have enough problems. You'll do me a favor if you leave right now. Go on!"

He opened the metal curtain just enough for Serafín to crawl out, like a small animal escaping from a trap about to spring.

◆　◆　◆　◆

Serafín went into the depth of night. He was suffocating but felt that if he stopped moving, grief would catch up and sink its fangs into him like a wild boar.

"Where are you going, Serafín?"

By now the streets were dark and empty, completely empty, with holes in the pavement and stretches of pure dirt. Only the cold was rattling around.

"Stop, Serafín. Ask somebody where the street with palm trees is."

"There's nobody here, Mamá. Nobody."

◆ ◆ ◆ ◆

He had been in a deserted place once before, but with the advantage that it was not nighttime. Although when it's so empty, it feels almost the same, by day or by night, whether in that small village near Aguichapan or in Mexico City. He arrived with his papá one morning, but the people had gone on one of those long pilgrimages and there was no market. Only a few people had stayed scattered around as if trying to hide the shame of being so few.

"Damned people," Papá said to the man who had explained it to him, smoking on the corner with his foot set squarely against the wall. "So much walking for this." And he let the maguey bag with the sombreros fall to the ground.

"I didn't go. What for? A complete loss of time. Right?"

They started talking and Serafín crossed the empty plaza with the dry fountain, cracked benches, and a few capulin trees swaying in the wind, as if by the sadness of solitude.

When he turned around, he no longer saw his papá, and there felt the same sensation that had not come back until now, in Mexico City. He walked down a stone-paved street with white rock dust that reawakened his desire to cry. He walked the distance of the whole street and got to the end of the village, where the houses were flimsy and blackened, made of tin and wood. Because he felt so nervous he knocked on a door, but no one answered. Looking through the bare windows, he saw a few pieces of dusty furniture and something like the shadows of the people who lived there. Instead of having gone on a pilgrimage, they seem to have died, and the shadows did not leave the bodies. They were the souls themselves.

He sat down for a moment on a stone trough and started to cry. Everything he saw was menacing him with its solitude—the wide, yellow expanse of cornfields, the hill of huisaches and mesquites, a tree right in front of him shedding tears of resin.

He went back to the plaza by the same street. An old woman in a rebozo was saying her rosary, making a noise like the droning of bees in a flower. He asked her about his papá.

"Who is your papá, child? There's hardly anyone in the village today. Look, even the church is closed. Only the really old people or the really lazy ones are still here."

"My papá was with a man, but suddenly they disappeared."

"Then they probably went to the cantina. But no, the cantina is also closed. They must be in some house drinking."

"And what shall I do?"

"Sit here close to me. If we pray together, you'll feel calmer."

"Maybe my papá went back to Aguichapan." And fear welled up in his throat, in the voice that went deep inside him.

"Without you? No father would do that. He has to be drinking in some house. When men don't have anything to do, they always drink. If he's trying to find you, he'll come to the plaza. Give me your hand, like this."

And in a while his papá found him there, sleeping on the old woman's lap.

♦ ♦ ♦ ♦

"I'm with you, Serafín. Don't give up. The sun will be coming up soon."

"But I'm very cold, Mamá. And very sleepy. I can't go on with the sleepiness and the pain in my stomach."

"Go back to your father. It's better for you to spend tonight there."

"I don't even know where the store is anymore. And the glow I saw a little while ago has gone farther away from me instead of getting closer."

"But in that street you're not going to find anything or anyone or anywhere to sleep."

"I'm going to sit down on the sidewalk for a little bit. I really can't keep going."

"If you sit down, you're going to go to sleep, Serafín, and the cold will get you. Keep on walking. You'll see the sun really will come up soon."

"For a little while. Don't you think that glow is just a mirage, Mamá? Maybe part of the night itself."

"It's probably not as far away as you think."

"I saw it getting farther away all the time, even though I was running toward it."

"Don't go to sleep, Serafín."

"I'm just going to close my eyes to rest them."

"Serafín, forgive me."

"Forgive you for what, Mamá?"

But the voices, also, were dissolving in the rising tide of deepest sleep.